Also by David Gilmour

Back on Tuesday
An Affair with the Moon
Lost Between Houses

How Boys See Girls

Vintage Canada
A Division of Random House of Canada

DAVID GILMOUR

*How
Boys
See
Girls*

Originally published in hardcover in Canada in 1991 by
Random House of Canada Limited, Toronto.

Grateful acknowledgement is made to Warner/Chappell
Music Inc., for permission to reprint excerpts from "Baby I'm
a Star" by Prince Nelson. Copyright © 1984 by Controversy
Music. All rights on behalf of Controversy Music for the
U.S.A. and Canada administered by WB Music Corp. All
rights reserved. Reprinted by permission of Warner/Chappell
Music, Inc.

Canadian Cataloguing in Publication Data

Gilmour, David, 1949-
  How boys see girls

I. Title.

PS8563.I56H69 1992   C813'.54   C92-094642-9
PR9199.3.G55H69 1992

Cover illustration: Blair Drawson
Cover design: Mike Lam
Printed and bound in the United States of America

ISBN 978-0-394-22299-8

To Maggie Huculak with love

How Boys See Girls

1

I was drinking a lot in those days. I don't apologize for it. You have to do something to make yourself feel better and for a while there it worked. When the booze clicked in, things looked ripe as yellow flowers and the moment soared like one of those free-floating birds I saw from the hotel window when I was a kid.

In those days I hung out in a bar called the Circus. I went in for a drink one day and I never came out.

I loved it. I loved watching the waitresses slide through the cinnamon puddles of light. Across the bar from my stool was a tinted wall-length mirror and most times, particularly after dark, I liked to watch my reflection. Sometimes it turned ugly, even monstrous, but other times it was . . . handsome, and I found that comforting.

The owner was gangster good-looking, a man in his early

fifties. He looked as if he should have been running a hotel casino in Puerto Rico. His name was Vic and he had the instincts of an animal, very close to the surface. He didn't know what I was—or so I fancied. He intuited there was nothing I could do for him yet he liked me. It puzzled both of us.

Sometimes he'd come behind the bar, shoot the breeze in a slow, deep-chested voice. Maybe he'd buy me a drink. That was rare.

Some nights I went home with a waitress or a customer. Failed writers exude a kind of plagiarized weariness. For some young girls, who haven't smelt it before, it's a potent musk.

One night Vic said to me: "You're a bright guy. You don't want to spend all your life in here." He gestured to the room.

He had a point. But so did I. The truth was: there was nowhere else I wanted to be more. I was happy there.

I didn't want to spend time with my speech writer colleagues. I had more talent than they did, crates more talent, and I hated talking shop as if we were equals.

Let me put it this way. Every time I got a new job or a new girlfriend or a new anything, I'd look up after a while and I'd see the ceiling about four inches over my head. The Circus was the only place where I knew, I absolutely knew, that when I looked up, I'd see the sky.

I didn't intend to spend "all my life" in the Circus. I was doing what I was supposed to be doing. Something was going to happen to me, I was sure of it. I didn't know what it was yet but I knew that just like some great green wave it was going to thunder past the Circus one day and suck me right out the door.

I believed in it.

Of course there were dark periods, hangovers so bad I was afraid to leave the house until after dark, when I expected perfect strangers to punch me in the face. There were blackouts; unfortunately they were never complete. I'd only remember the bad stuff: coming on sloppy to a woman in whose eyes you could read sudden disappointment.

I found an embossed ashtray beside the bed. I couldn't remember where I'd stolen it.

I had a self-inflicted nightmare that one morning I was going to find a dead body in the next room. Or wake up and find my front teeth missing.

Those were the "off" moments.

Drinking took me wonderful places, but sometimes during the course of a weekend binge things went wrong, a harsh word, an inexplicable flare-up with someone over something.

These were the rare moments.

During the week I wrote speeches, often hungover, but it didn't matter. I was good and I could always get a politician quoted in the morning papers.

Some nights I'd start at the Circus and drink my way home. I'd stop at the Brass Hat for a stand-up beer with Harry Chillum. Although he was my age, his hair had gone completely white. He carried a forty-ounce bottle of Finlandia in his shoulder bag and like clockwork every twenty minutes he disappeared into the bathroom for a private slug.

It didn't matter if he was broke or I was buying. That's how he liked to drink. Then I'd move on to the roof of the Park Plaza. Spolin was often there, sitting near the window overlooking the northern part of the city. He was a good-looking, sharp-featured man with the booming laugh of an actor at a friend's performance. Somebody had once told him the Park Plaza was a writers' bar—it had been, in the '50s—so he came there to write his novel and wait to be disturbed.

"I'm working," he'd say, just to be sure you took his writing seriously, and then he'd invite you to sit down. He was thirty-one. His mother paid his rent and he was very prickly about it.

"The best thing about fame," he told me once, "is that you get to tell everybody to fuck off."

Maybe I'd stop by the Other Cafe; my ex-wife came looking for me there sometimes. If she wasn't there, I'd order a Caesar salad to go. I'd save it for later. I didn't want to stink in case I ran into a woman in the next block or two. On the way home I'd turn down a side street and poke my head into the red gloom of Sangra's, a Portuguese bar where I drank Bloody Marys and fell in love with that South African girl fifteen years ago. I have a superstition about her, that she and I aren't finished with each other, that someday she'll come back and when she does she'll come looking for me in that bar. Sometimes I think she was the only woman I ever really loved. No, not loved. Wanted. When she left me, I wanted her dead.

The glass pane in my front door rattles in its frame as I go up the stairs. I check my answering service for messages. I stare out the window at the booby hatch across the street. On the fourth floor, the lights are always on.

I turn off the kitchen light and walk down the hall and get into bed. I roll over on my right side, put my hand under the pillow and go to sleep.

Years ago, an ex-girlfriend told me about a disastrous affair she'd once had with a coke-shooting, gun-toting kid from Kansas City. One day he said to her, "Honey, I wish I could shrink you down to the size of my thumb and put you in my pocket and carry you around all day. That way I'd never have to be away from you." She found that scarier than needles, even firearms, and she fled north.

But you know, style aside, I kind of know what he meant, this snow-crazed boy from Kansas. Because I felt that way about Holly.

The first time I saw her on the street it filled me with extraordinary despair, despair that such a creature existed in the world and that I might never fuck her. God only gives you the things you *sort* of want. Never the big stuff. That way he makes sure you stay till the end of the party.

There's nothing very interesting about the corner of Yonge and Bloor Streets. It's not pretty or dramatic; it has no history, no signature to speak of, but it's always struck me as the center of Toronto, the emotional center. A second-rate men's clothing shop and a glassed-in fast food joint hold down the south corners; on the north, a black-windowed skyscraper and a beige tower. In their shade is a string of rag-tag street vending tables. Students, tanned and slumming, sell watches and cotton T-shirts and macrame belts and ivory chess pieces, good stuff mixed indiscriminately with junk, mass-produced and glittering in the hot sun.

But there's a feeling at this corner, not so much for what is here, but for what is close. A feeling that everyone in the city must pass this corner, that they have or are or will again soon. A bicycle courier sluices through the pedestrians and shoots off down the street, pumped up as a prizefighter. At the crosswalk, a paunchy, barrel-chested film critic sails across the street, full of himself. A smart, sexy, sixtyish woman follows him. She reminds me of Eva Marie Saint. Then a young girl with a weak chin wearing an ill-advised wide-brimmed Spanish hat. A smart couple, tennis rackets on their backs, on their way to the health club, and after them, a tough-looking man with a tottering Parkinson's walk. A Jamaican boy stops at the corner, whistles, looks about with aggressive boredom. A white man wearing a wig comes to a stop beside him and puts down his briefcase, then catches sight of the black boy and discreetly reaches down and picks up the briefcase. A sideburned cowboy slumps by, looking for something not here anymore. Students, office girls, self-satisfied young lawyers talking in clipped tones, they all pass here.

And then there's the exciting possibility that someone will come along, a beautiful woman, a thrilling encounter which will take you out of your life. Somewhere, as Baudelaire said, out of this world. I have always felt a quickening of the pulse when I approach this corner—in spite of the fact that nothing happens here, that the people I run into are only people I don't want to see, a friend I had a boozy tiff with, an old professor who held such high hopes for me.

Except, of course, for this one time. That was the payoff. That'll keep me coming back for a lifetime.

It was a dreary, overcast April afternoon, prematurely humid. People were in shirts and short sleeves; they carried sweaters and jackets thrown over their shoulders. I was on my way to the department store to buy a refrigerator. I stopped at a cluster of street vending tables, peering at this and that— lambskin slippers, a black Chanel sweatshirt—when, a couple of tables away, a girl in a red sleeveless shirt lifted a bare arm and unconsciously, almost sleepily, scratched the damp hair underneath while she talked absently to a male customer. I stood transfixed, in a kind of nauseated trance. I wanted to put my tongue there; I wanted to hold her wrist over her head and lick the sweat from under her arm; taste the salt on my tongue. I wanted to lead her to the restaurant across the street and take her down that scuffed white staircase and into the bathroom and do the most extraordinarily intimate things to her.

It was a terrible, terrible, terrible feeling.

Then she put her arm down.

I examined the wares of the other street vendors. I can't remember what I saw. I may have been looking at glistening silver rings or watches or loaded guns. I don't know. My heart was beating like mad, like I'd been poisoned and it was trying to flush me clean. I was afraid even to look up because of what I imagined would be so plainly written on my face.

Abruptly, it began to rain. The vendors closed their tables and scurried for shelter under the awning of a bank. I followed them. It was cramped under that awning: it smelt of warm, summer bodies pressed together. I stood behind Holly. She sat with her chin in her hand. Someone, a boy, tried to talk to her. I looked down at her brown neck and arms. The sun had been good to those arms. She must have felt me staring at her because she turned around. A small, schoolgirl's face regarded me expressionlessly. Delicate, pretty features, a sharp chin, a sharp nose; short hair dark with perspiration.

She's too pretty, I thought. No one that pretty could possibly want me to do all the things I want to do to her.

For a split second I held her glance but my nerve collapsed and I looked away. The moment was gone. She stared balefully out into the traffic, the umbrellas, the grey depression of a city closing up like a flower in the rain.

It rained and rained and it was making me unhappy to stand there. She didn't look back again; she mustn't have seen any reason to. I grew bored. The rain dripped down the awning, a cluster of drops fell on her forearm. She looked a long time into the traffic before she seemed to notice. There was, about her, a sleepy, indifferent passivity that made me ache. She looked at that little splash on her arm, didn't brush it off; then she looked away again.

I stepped around her. I took a small sideways peek, I wanted to see her breast through the arm of her shirt. I did; it just made me unhappier. Then I hurried off into the rain, imagining, I think, snickers from the rain-huddled street vendors, among whom sat the girl with the brown arms and the water splash dripping down her elbow. But there was nothing but the rain and the hopeless swish of wet tires on pavement. I walked for blocks.

Later that afternoon, I was in the Circus when I saw her walk by with her vending table. I hurried out on the street. I watched her walk all the way to Bay Street, that funny toes-out walk. The next time I saw her, I swore to myself, I'd talk to her.

Actually it was because of her that I went to the Zanzibar. It was hot, sensual weather, a day for watching women, and I was walking slowly up Yonge Street. I was thinking about her, this girl selling jewelry. I stopped in front of the Zanzibar. Now I never go to places like that, I'm too vain. But sometimes just being near sex is better than not having any at all. I wanted to sit in a dark place, think about her and watch a woman take her clothes off.

Inside the Zanzibar, a bass guitar throbbed. Ventilators jetted foul, beer-stale breath onto the street. It is a smell I have always hated. It means a big, noisy, windowless room where you have to shout, a shithole where a midget greets you at the door, a fat lady sings flat and everybody tells you the joint's got charm.

Over the door, a sign. GIRLS, GIRLS, GIRLS. Two men rushed across Yonge Street, jackets open, ties flapping, hamburgers in their hands, and went inside.

I followed them.

There was no midget at the door. Worse, a blond, frizzy-haired bouncer in his mid-twenties. The kind of short-fuse psycho with a weapons collection in the attic of his mom's house. He was wearing a tuxedo shirt and a red cummerbund. It was a surprise he could muster the IQ to wear it fat side forward.

"You fuckin' tall guys drive me nuts," he said.

The Zanzibar. Thick, smoky air; a roomful of pale white faces wavering in the dingy air. It reminded me of those strange sea snakes who dig their tails into the ocean floor, washed to and fro in the warm currents. A Marilyn Monroe lookalike surveyed the room from a balcony stretched across the top of the stage.

Young men in work clothes sat at tables of two and ordered rum and Cokes. A short-sleeved accountant nursed a beer and did his homework under the cash register light, ticking expertly on a small adding machine.

It was pitch black inside, and it took a while to get used to the darkness. Dim red bulbs flickered overhead.

The blue-lit stage was empty; there was a peekaboo shower, a Plexiglas cage near the deejay's booth. It was backlit like an aquarium.

Now, what goes on in there, I wondered.

Prince and the Revolution boomed, thumped and funked:

Hey look me over,
Tell me, do you like what you see?

Four white-haired gentlemen took the table next to mine. In their drab suits they looked like low-ranking Russian civil servants. A single overweight man with small, shiny, intelligent eyes sat on my other side. Table dancers glided down the aisle, trying to catch my eye.

A disc jockey appeared, a paunchy black man in a leopard skin vest. He flipped a switch and tapped the microphone. "Testes, one, two, three," he said. "Testes, one, two, three."

God. Another Nobel candidate.

"Now, ladies and gentlemen, the tiny, the sweet, the delectable Girl in the Baseball Cap, Tabitha!"

The house lights dimmed. A snare drum snapped, a bass drum whapped, the boys blew the spit from their trumpets and then *honk!* A slender stem of a woman, a gamine really, appeared at the edge of the stage. She wore a string bikini, topped by a sweatshirt sporting the word SEXY in sparkly letters. She wore a baseball cap with the beak to the side. She had high cheekbones, sunken cheeks, a face fashioned with a sculptor's hatchet. She had the body of a young boy. I ordered beer from a waitress in a starched tuxedo shirt.

The wall speakers burped as the bass line kicked in, weaving, jabbing, jumping in and out of the snare drum. Into the furnace came the congas, ringing like metal pipes.

Tabitha spun across the stage, marking a spot on the wall, snapping her head around to catch it before it fell to the ground. Spin, spot, spin, spot, spin, spot. No smiles for this girl. She came sternly to the front of the stage, opened the crotch of her bikini, let the four Soviet octogenarians have a peek, then covered up again.

Out came the blanket. She did a slow, careful head stand, legs apart, then flipped neatly over into the splits. She laid her beautiful, baseball-capped head on her arms and pretended to fall asleep.

Why, it was just like Swan Lake. Sort of, I don't know, hand-in-your-pants classy.

She lifted up her sweatshirt, up over the flat stomach, over a bony rib cage, slowly upward. The entire room craned its neck.

She held it right at her nipples, then swept it over her head and dropped it in a bundle at her feet. A hand reached from the pit. It wanted the shirt. So did I. It wanted to take it away somewhere dark. So did I.

Tabitha glared down at the hand and it scuttled away.

She spun around. Rubbed her breasts.

"Ah," said we in the audience, "so that's what girls do when they're alone."

She took us in with comic-book bewilderment: What are *you* doing here?

I chuckled. It was all too ridiculous. But I didn't leave and I didn't take my eyes off the stage.

Off came the bikini bottoms. Wearing only her baseball cap, Tabitha stood stark naked and childlike in front of us. I had an awful feeling I was getting a hard-on, a real dribbler. And getting a hard-on in that place, well, it's just not how I saw myself turning forty. I used to feel sorry for people who came to these places.

Tabitha opened the door of the shower. This could get interesting. With a fleeting, "naughty" glance back at us, she went inside. She turned a knob and by God, we were in the shower. Tabitha was going to have a shower and we were going to watch her. She squirted the hose against the inside of the

Plexiglas—it was starting to steam up—and then, when the glass was drippy wet and clear as a bell, she pressed her little bum against it—a tiny, glazed pressed ham. Furtively I slipped a hand in my pants and felt the very end of my cock. Just research, mind you. I was, after all, a writer. A tiny little betraying drop slid out. I confess I was in no hurry to take my hand out, either.

I looked around. Perfect. There I was, playing with myself in a strip joint. Perhaps it's true: a man's character is his destiny.

Tabitha was now giving herself a douche. She was washing and scrubbing and rinsing, giving us peekaboo glances over her shoulder. (Ah, so that's what girls do in the shower.)

Little Tabitha stepped triumphantly out of the steam. A towel flew through the air from off stage. She caught it with a damp hand. I headed to the bathroom. I walked along the runway, past Tabitha, alarmed for a second that she knew where—and why—I was going. As I went down the stairs I got a final glimpse of her: She was tying her feet together with a black scarf and trying to hang herself upside down from a hook on the back wall.

I clipped quickly down the stairs, past the Marilyn Monroe double arguing on the phone with her baby-sitter, and slipped into the bathroom. It smelt of disinfectant and was surprisingly clean, but there was something in the sink. I went over and looked. It was a blood-soaked towel, the blood fresh and bright red. It kind of spoilt the mood, but I went into the stall anyway. I locked the door and sat down and took out my cock. It had lost a little of its steam on the trip downstairs. I gave it a few ruminative tugs, but I couldn't get the image of the bloody towel out of my mind.

I closed my eyes and thought about Tabitha, by now, no doubt, hung like a chicken from the ceiling. No dice. I switched films. I thought about the girl on the street, the jewelry vendor, her arms raised behind her head. It was over in seconds.

I zipped up and went outside. It was the first time, all day, I felt free of her.

2

A week later I was sitting on the porch of my house in Chinatown. It was a fine spring day. The trees had lost their unhappy winter starkness; almost overnight they had bloomed. Dandelions dotted my lawn. A slight wind stirred the sheets on the line. The leaves on the trees rustled and turned silver like a school of fish changing direction. The air was full of sounds: from a backyard, a hammer banged on a window frame; a dog barked in an alley. My downstairs neighbor, Mr. Foo, talked in Cantonese to his wife and tinkered in his small garden, a handkerchief on his head. A cat slunk along the sidewalk and turned up a front walk, disappearing in cool porch shadows. A plump black bird squawked and flew from his tree. It was a lovely, easy day, the sky blue and cloud-dusted, and I was only partially aware that I could be happier.

Suddenly a white Honda turned the corner sharply and gunned down my street, disturbing the peace. But then that too passed and torpor reasserted itself. A stout woman dressed in mourning black—Italian, Sicilian, Greek, I couldn't tell —passed in front of my house. Behind her was Holly. It seemed providential, her turning up like that. Only moments before, I'd been having idle sexual daydreams about her.

She walked right by my house. I half rose to my feet. But I didn't speak to her. I couldn't—I'd left it too long—and I watched her boyish, bouncy walk, toes pointed ever so slightly outwards, all the way down the street. I was sure she'd turn around, but she didn't. She didn't even look to the side. (That was very Holly.) She just kept going, a bare-armed girl in a bobbing cloth cap.

For a week after I saw her on my street, I woke up every morning thinking about her. But I didn't go looking for her. I was waiting for something good to happen to me, a good job, a blinding piece of luck. Then I'd go over and hop up and down in front of her. But it didn't happen.

I turned forty. Then my uncle died. His wife pushed him down the stairs—she did it every six months—but this time it croaked him. Don't think I'm going to get sentimental. He was a spineless prick, he looked like an overstuffed trout, and he got what he deserved.

But he was rich and I had my fingers crossed. Maybe he'd left something for me. I'd been down that road before. My grandfather was the vice president of Shell Oil of New Jersey, but my mother, damn her, got herself disinherited when she was nineteen for marrying a race car driver who drank himself to death. He wasn't my father but sometimes I think he should have been.

Anyway, I like funerals; it's how my family keeps in touch.

They're more fun than weddings although I'm not sure why. Death makes a lot of things forgivable and at a funeral, you can really fuck up and get away with it. You can fall on your face in the punch bowl, it looks like grief. You can burst into tears talking about someone you never gave a shit about: it makes you look good, like a real man who's not afraid to show his feelings.

And besides, after a few drinks, you can come on to just about anybody you want.

Well, not anybody. That's what I found out.

I didn't bother with the service. It was a late afternoon affair way the hell at the edge of the city. Anyway, they're always a bore; you can't talk, you can't drink beforehand; you just end up sitting in the back row, scanning the bowed heads, trying to figure out who you want to fuck.

So I went straight from the gym to the reception; freshly showered, I rubbed my hands together with anticipation. If worse came to worst, it'd be a first-rate piss-up. A little after seven, I ate a ham sandwich to take on some ballast and took a taxi up to Forest Hill. We drove through the city, past a giant, tragic house that looked like a toy castle. We crossed a bridge; a green park fell away below. A red-haired girl walked a dog at the very lip of the forest. The cab moved along shaded streets, past an oval park where a Filipino woman waited for a bus; puttered slowly along a hundred-yard stretch of mansions, red brick, beige, green putty, candy pink, no two houses the same. Down the street, a police car guarded the house of the American consul. A priest glided by in a four-wheel drive. We stopped in front of a stone-grey mansion. A red Mercedes rested in the early evening cool. This was—and still is, no doubt—the home of my uncle's son, a keep-fit asshole, Mr. Eddie Grogan and his wife, a former Miss Arizona, Ivy. Like their parents, the Grogans were dreadful people, liars and drunks, but oddly enough, they had two remarkable children, sweet-natured, lovely kids.

They were twin girls, about eight years old. I hadn't seen them for years but when I spotted them shaking hands and curtsying in the foyer, my heart went out to them; I wondered how long it would be before their parents ruined them.

There was also a baby-sitter staying at the house. It was Holly.

I went straight to the bar and gulped down a double Russian vodka. Then I took another look at her. She wore a dark blue cotton dress—thank God it had sleeves—small gold earrings, no makeup. She was occupied talking to a large man in a brown suit and bow tie but she must have sensed something because, quite abruptly, she turned her face toward me. Its sharp-featured beauty startled me and I dropped my glance. I believe I was actually frightened of her. For the first time I felt enormous sympathy for that poor prick in *Death in Venice*. I used to think he was just a silly old fruitcake who'd stayed out in the sun too long.

She had the smooth skin under her eyes that young girls have.

I walked away into the kitchen, somewhere I didn't have to look at her. Maybe I couldn't get her. Maybe, when I talked to her, she wouldn't have the least notion why. Just a nice old guy her dad's age. Maybe, if I bent over to kiss her, she would cringe with confusion, then embarrassment.

"I'm sorry. I must have misunderstood."

How mortifying.

But I couldn't resist. I came back out and had another Moskovskaya. I was already feeling a little woolly-headed.

Oh well, at least I wasn't coming on to my daughter's little friends. Not yet, anyway. I congratulated myself on that.

But these were hardly the things I should be thinking about at a funeral. There was the estate. So far, not a raised eyebrow in my direction.

Other cars arrived; cousins, uncles, strange, gaunt relatives from small towns with unhappy names: Galt, Whitby, Burnhamthorpe.

I checked the baby-sitter again. She bent over to whisper into a small, eager ear. To torture myself I checked to see how much of her dress she filled out. This was obscene. I contemplated going to the upstairs bathroom to fix myself up. God, this girl was turning me into a monkey. There had to be some other way of dealing with her.

I went back to the bar and got another double. My hands were shaking. I'd quite forgotten why I was there.

Then I caught sight of my brittle-boned aunt. She was sitting in a straight-backed chair, a tall rum and Coke in her hand. I looked at her spindly fingers, imagined them sliding up soundlessly behind my uncle at the head of the stairs. I wondered if she watched him tumble or whether she scurried away. They were killer's hands. Amusingly enough, a man I didn't recognize came up at that moment, took one of those hands and touched his lips ever so slightly to it. She was hideously made-up, her lips puckered like a rosy red asshole. Caligula's mom.

I crossed the thick carpet to extend my condolences. "Aunt Jane," I said, looking for a glimmer of recognition.

"Bix," she said. Her eyes were boozy bloodshot. "You look more and more like your mother every year. Especially here, around your mouth." She touched a fingernail to my lips. "How I miss your mother. I loved her so much. Do you think she's happy?"

I nodded and smiled. My mother had been dead for many years.

"I'm so dreadfully sorry about Uncle James," I said. Then, wrinkling my brow with concern, I lowered my voice. "How did it happen?"

"He fell down the stairs," she said gravely.

"What—again?"

Her eyes pinpointed like a hawk's.

I shook my head in a gesture of sad bewilderment. Her eyes softened slightly. But not entirely.

"Of course," she said, "he forgave you for not paying him back."

"But Aunt Jane, I did."

She looked down, closed her eyes and shook her head crisply. "No," she said, simply and correctly. "Not all of it."

"He told me to forget about the rest."

But she moved on. She had scored her point. It was those kinds of axe blows, a million little chippings-away, that had driven her own now-brain-damaged son, the other one, to a suicide attempt in the garage. It had also, I remembered with some pride, provoked my mother into tossing a full glass of red wine in her face over dinner.

But there was no mention of James's estate.

Eddie joined us. He was a muscular bonehead who played golf, loved to hunt and couldn't make his wife come. I couldn't look at him without remembering that. It always made me smile, in spite of my good manners. Ivy'd told me the story years ago, as she drove me home after a family do. She'd had quite a bit to drink, and I'm not sure to this day if she remembers. The story had a sad tag though. Ivy left him once for a summer and took up with a doctoral student (Faulkner) who, like his subject, was a keen stick man; but more important, a generous one, and early in their affair, it may have been the first night after a movie and a beer, he gave her a blow job that turned on all the lights on the Christmas tree. For two months Ivy couldn't sit down to read the newspaper without the grad student going down on her. And yet—and this is the killer, there's a message here somewhere—at summer's end, when Eddie closed up the cottage, Ivy went back to him. And the lights on the Christmas tree never came on again.

Eddie hated me. Thought I was an effete smart-ass. He had the explosive, paranoid vanity of the aging athlete. Some years ago, I'd teased him about his tummy at a Christmas party, I even gave it a playful pinch, and he got so mad he made a lunge for me. Somebody stopped him. Lucky thing, too. He would have beaten the shit out of me.

Eddie wedged himself protectively between me and his mother. He stood just a little too close to you. It was an act of asserted power, both aggressive and vaguely, off-puttingly sexual.

"It's a damn sad thing," I said.

Eddie stared coolly at me. "Please don't swear in my house."

It caught Jane off guard. She had a foul mouth herself; a few fingers of Barbadian rum and she turned the air blue. "Don't be ridiculous, dear. You break the law all the time."

I glanced over and noticed the two young girls trickling into the crowded living room.

"Your children are exquisite," I said. "Who's the baby-sitter?"

Eddie glanced sharply at me. "Holly Briggs," he said carefully. One of the little girls whispered something into Holly's ear. Then, taking a child in each hand, she retreated up a long carpeted flight of stairs. I checked the time. Jane handed her empty glass to Eddie and he pushed his way across the room to fill it. It was now eight-thirty. Shadows grew chilly, the sky a soft pearl pink.

I went back to the bar. The bartender, a rangy blond kid, took ostentatious peeks at *An Actor Prepares*. I ordered another double and a cold beer. I waited for Holly to come back downstairs. I'm not sure how much time elapsed. The party drifted onto the patio. A child fell into the pool. The neon bug zapper murdered mosquitoes with a faint crackle. The family cat caught a bird and ate it guiltily in the bushes. If you listened carefully, you could hear the tiny bones crack.

I went upstairs. I walked slowly down the hall. I could hear the ice cubes rattle in my glass; the sound of the party slugged its way dimly up the stairs. I went into the bathroom. I shut the door. I looked at myself in the mirror. I was getting slammed. My face had that beefy, thick look, particularly when I smiled.

I washed my face and took a piss. I opened the medicine cabinet and checked through the prescription bottles for anything that might be fun. Nothing too interesting. At the very back, under a tampon box, I found a tiny, dusty vial. I gave it a shake. Something rattled. I nudged it open. Valium. I shook a couple into my palm and tossed them back with a glass of water.

I was going to put the vial back, but then I remembered I was going to have a very bad hangover the following morning, so I dropped it into my breast pocket and gave it a pat.

Then I heard a door open. I stood very still, staring into the mirror. I practically put my finger to my lips. I peeked out. Holly carried a stack of crisp sheets and a pillow down the hall. Aware that something hummed in the air, she looked over her shoulder. Seeing me, she smiled and disappeared into a bedroom.

I closed the door again. I waited there for ten minutes. I was loaded, I admit it, but I was hoping she would come after me. I closed my eyes and tried to put the thought in her head. I wrinkled my brow, I concentrated on her, I tried to suck her back into the hall. Then I opened the door.

Holly Briggs stood right in front of the door. I stepped toward her. But something was wrong. She lowered her glance, I put my hand on her elbow, her face brushed clumsily against my chest and kept on going, right around me. All the way around and into the bathroom. There was confused laughter and then, with a furtive glance, she shut the door. I heard the toilet seat clank down. I had left it up. And probably, for the first time in my life, since I was four anyway, I'd forgotten to flush the toilet. Or had I?

Droop-tailed, I retreated downstairs and waited for her to come down. The brush had sobered me up, or so I thought, and I asked the bartender for a martini. I moved deeper into dark waters. I have a vague, sweat-inducing memory of speaking French to someone, I don't recall who. I seemed to be having difficulty making myself understood in any language. I have a distinct memory of Eddie shooting me an impatient go-home! glance, but it rolled off my rubberized shoulders. At one point, I stood rather dramatically at the foot of the stairs and looked up. The Valium and the booze gusted me even farther out to sea. A muffled voice told me to go home immediately. I ignored it. I put my hand on the banister, I put a foot on the lowermost stair, the rest seemed to take care of itself. I climbed the stairs. I stopped in front of Holly's door. I slipped off my shoes. I wavered ever so slightly on my heels, then caught my balance. I went in.

I shut the door behind me.

"Holly," I said to the feathery darkness. I heard a sheet rustle. Then, for reasons I still don't understand, I lay down on the floor. Perhaps I was waiting for her to come to me, perhaps I forgot where I was, perhaps the Valium kicked in a final, lethal notch. I don't know. I undid my shirt, I was too stoned to take it off. I undid my pants. I opened my fly. I closed my eyes and then I drifted off.

Somewhere in the mists a sharp pain woke me up. At first I thought I was dreaming but there it was again, a sharp, eye-watering pinch to my waist. And then all hell broke loose. In the blinding light he came straight at me, his arms stiff. I jumped to my feet, my hands covering myself. He grabbed me by the throat; he slipped a leg behind me and I crashed to the floor.

That's when I saw them: two children in matching pink nightshirts stared wide-eyed at me from their bunk bed.

Eddie Grogan hauled me to my feet like a rag doll and shook me.

"Don't!" I said. And suddenly Eddie knew. He knew I'd got the wrong room, he knew I wasn't after his kids. But he was drunk, he had the fury of the self-righteous, he had a small audience and he had someone he could beat up. He cocked back his fist and chopped me hard in the mouth. I could taste the blood. But it didn't stop there. He frog-marched me down the stairs. He yanked open the front door and shoved me outside. The door slammed. I did up my pants, my hands shaking like mad. The door opened again. I stepped back. A pair of running shoes banged off my chest. On the second floor, something moved behind a curtain.

It was Holly.

/3

*I*t was a sunshiny afternoon a couple of weeks later, the light very bright and shallow, the sidewalks teeming with the unemployed and the aged. As if the booby hatches were airing out their summer catch. I was on my way over to the Pink Palace, the House of Legislature, to tape-record a Minister for whom I was writing my annual speech on the "Renaissance of Canadian Film." I hadn't written for this guy before. He was "folksy," I was told. I wanted to know how folksy. All week long I'd tried to get access, just five minutes with him, so I could hear his voice, get an idea of his speech patterns. Did he use images, jokes, had he ever read a book and so on. But for reasons best known to himself he never got around to calling me so I headed over for a post-luncheon session with a tape recorder. He was giving a statement at 2:35, his press agent assured me. I was late, but I knew he'd be later.

Just in front of the fruit market I looked up and there was Holly walking toward me, also in a hurry, clutching a large white sweater to her chest. She gave me a very warm, surprised smile, a smile I held onto right through the session until my boy finally came on at four-thirty. He had a monotone and no sense of humor whatsoever.

Later that night, I went to work on the speech. I started it with appropriate lameness: "There was a time when a Canadian film company, looked at closely, turned out to be no more than a letterhead and a rented station wagon."

I shook my head. I checked the delivery time. It was an after-dinner job. A boozy, sleepy audience, nursing a hard-on for the stenographer at the next table. I'd do them a favor going in. I'd make it brief.

Then, quite out of the blue, my ears began to hum. I had a premonition that something was going to happen. I became queasy with anticipation. It was as if I were getting the flu. I went into the kitchen. In the shadows of the park below, two drunks in overcoats, tanned and grizzled, nestled against each other like spoons and dozed. I imagined killing them, putting poison—rat poison—in a forty-ounce bottle of rye, leaving it beside them as a wake-up present. Croaking drunks in the park: I wondered if I was going mad.

Above them, above the trees, across the tram-tracked College Street, rose the grey stone-chested Clarke Institute of Psychiatry—and on the fourth floor a man, his hands behind his back, contemplated my house and the fading sunlight that moved across its face.

It was dark now, a soft spring evening. I followed a cramped back street behind my house, slipped between two narrow buildings, ran across College Street, leaving Chinatown and its shadowy porches behind, and crossed into the student quarter. A girl in a Swiss cape and sunglasses bicycled by. I took a shortcut through the university campus; walking toward me, cocky in a black leather jacket, a young man in his twenties—a boy really—a bandana around his head, dismissed me with an arrogant smirk. I cut across Queen's Park, past the statue of a black horse. A memory of my ex-wife Margaret and me, twenty years before, cavorting on that horse at six-thirty on a spring morning whizzed by like a shooting star, and I rushed on. I came out on a small deserted lane behind the Colonnade apartment buildings. And that's when I saw them. Holly and a dark-haired man walked a hundred feet ahead of me. He held her hand. Holly was wearing the white sweater. I darted back into a doorway. They stopped for a moment; she tugged up his sleeve and looked at his wristwatch. The gesture was alarmingly casual. Familiar. She must have seen him without his clothes on to know which wrist his watch was on. She must be fucking him.

They turned the corner and disappeared into the evening crowd on Bloor Street. Then I did something I had never done before. I followed them.

She let go of his hand. Irrationally, I wondered if this was for my sake. She kept that hand occupied, fiddling absent-mindedly with an earring. They walked on the south side, alongside the black wrought-iron gates that separated the lush green lawns of Philosophers' Walk. I trailed a hundred feet behind, on the north side, past the pizza house, the Chicken Chalet, Dunkin' Donuts, a rash of garish fast food joints, neon lit. It was not a pleasant juxtaposition, like a hyena tracking a pair of antelopes. I smelt blood. I smelt something unlike anything that had happened before about to happen.

They stopped at a crosswalk. I slipped into the foyer of an

Arabic restaurant. And then they went on, turning up a narrow, tree-arched street, Melrose Avenue. I followed them. There was that smell again, a salty, intimate odor like semen. It must have come from the leaves over my head. They were just disappearing into a driveway when I came out behind them. I walked very quickly across a dozen lawns, peeked around the corner of a house; for one second, tried to stop myself from stepping into the driveway, from going down that driveway and around the back of the house. But I didn't manage.

I knew what I wanted to see. I crept soundlessly along the brick wall of the house. Around the side, my jacket brushed the brick. The window was only a few feet in front of my face. It was open. A light was on. I heard voices. One was Holly's. There was a rattle in the kitchen; a water tap turned on. Then, very close to the window, the muffled squeak of a mattress taking the weight of a body. I heard her voice from the kitchen. The phone rang. She answered it. Her voice took on a formal, eager-to-please pitch. The conversation started with a lie. Holly said she was alone. Now why would a girl lie about a thing like that?

She hung up. There was an apologetic laugh. The room went dark; not quite dark, sort of watery with shadow. It took me a minute to figure it out. A candle. She had lit a candle.

Close to me, a faucet gleamed dull silver. This was creepy, I knew, but I couldn't stop myself. I put my foot on it and, taking hold of the underside of the windowsill, my arms shaking with the strain, pulled myself up. There in the middle of the bed, the dark-haired man knelt; he looked Mediterranean. Sculpture handsome. A thin muscular chest fell to a tight stomach. Two lines of tendons stretched down from there. Holly crouched in the candlelight, a beautiful girl in a blue-lit room. She cupped his balls in one hand, and gently, lovingly ran her encircled fingers down the shaft of his hardened cock, then lowered her mouth on it.

From my study, I could hear the sounds of children, hundreds of children, playing in the schoolyard across the street. The street gleamed in patches with spring puddles. A couple with a new baby passed me. I turned up King's College Road and into the university campus; a billboard advertised a symposium on semantics, a gay and lesbian nurses' night, a screening of Marlon Brando's *Burn!* On both sides, buildings, off-white and beige, rose into the blue spring sky: a metallurgy lab, a library; SLOW POKE REACTOR one sign said. Knots of students crossed a giant playing field; a girl carried a pair of white skates slung over her shoulder. On cold autumn days I still hunger for this place; hunger to buy new textbooks or sit in a drafty lecture hall, hunger for the sense of starting my life over again. But I don't go back. I know better.

I emerged from the shadows under the stone archway. A bright sun shone on my left. A cry from a touch football game floated across the playing fields. But I had to hurry. I was having lunch with my ex-wife Margaret. At least I think she's my ex-wife. When she divorced me, she never got around to paying the lawyer; so I have a suspicion that she and I are still married. That's just fine with me. I adore Margaret; I don't mind being married to her at all. Actually, it's flattering; she's done rather well for herself.

After she got rid of me, she did five years with a documentary filmmaker, a wiry, handsome man who fucked her on a lawn somewhere in Cuba. That's how she met him. Or so the story goes. She was drunk when she told me. But she dumped him too. He was a napper; he took naps in the afternoon. He did other naughty things: drank too much, sulked too much, fucked his best friend's wife on a visit home to Vancouver, but frankly that wasn't what got him chopped. It was the napping.

It's a moral thing with Margaret: Good people don't nap. It's that simple.

Anyway, like I said, she's done well for herself; she's good at running things. She ran an alternative school, then she ran a chain of theaters and now she's working for a minor film producer—a politician, really—who has a reputation for working with the kind of women who fight over who gets to make his plane reservations. I don't think it's going to work out.

But she's great company, a born conversationalist, even if she is a little bossy sometimes. After twenty years I can still blow a whole afternoon in a bar with her. It just goes poof, like that, and then it's dinner time. I cannot imagine what it is we talk about after all these years but it's like a magic well; it fills up every morning and we begin again.

Margaret was waiting for me at the Other Cafe, at a window table. She took off her sunglasses, her bright laughter infectious. I sat down with relish. It was going to be a fine afternoon. We ordered Heinekens. They arrived ice cold.

"Don't you simply love Heineken?" she gushed.

The talk turned to our daughter Zooey. We wondered at the length of her legs, her beautiful mouth, her animated intelligence, her gift for a well-turned phrase. We had many examples to consider.

"Really," I gasped, "the wonder of that child."

Suddenly there was a knock on the glass window. Margaret turned a sunglassed face to see who it was; it was Holly. Margaret gave her a glance, dismissive and barely patient. She didn't like to be interrupted when she was talking, particularly by a street urchin who might be fucking her ex-husband. It was all too tiresome.

Holly gestured for me to join her on the sidewalk. She didn't look well. A small cold sore burned on her upper lip. It made her self-conscious.

"I want to see you," she said. "Do you know where I live?"

Pause.

"No."

"Yes you do. I saw you."

I must have looked panic stricken.

"I don't mind," she said.

When I sat back down again, I was visibly excited. Margaret gave me a long, cool look of appraisal; she wanted me to know simply that she knew, that she had missed nothing, but it wasn't a subject—or, from the looks of things, a girl—that interested her. She hated my taste in women, always had; even when we were in university she used to laugh up her sleeve and make jokes about them, never let me bring them into her apartment.

Margaret believed, sometimes it was her undoing, that if you ignored unpleasant traits in people you liked, they got better.

I was going to wait a couple of days to go and see Holly, make it look as if I had something else to do. But I was too impatient and that same night around midnight, after I'd sobered up from my day with Margaret, I jumped out of bed and rushed over. It was damp and humid on Melrose Avenue. Men in unbuttoned shirts took in the night air. I passed a park where three Indians were overturning a swing set; past a brightly lit window where, framed in yellow tones as in a movie, a woman talked on the phone. Then, from the third floor of a dark house across the street, the sound of typing, fast and inspired. Dry-mouthed, I turned over in my head the things I'd say if she was not alone.

Holly Briggs lived in an elegant, brown brick house near the top of her street, just up from a Catholic girls' school. I used to live on that street myself, years ago, very close to Holly's place, with a lisping creative writing student who later moved west, wrote a prize-winning, unreadable novel in which, dear me, she painted a most unflattering portrait of our love time together. I tried to remember which apartment we tortured each other in, but I couldn't.

I went to the front door. A bicycle was locked to a post on the veranda. I looked at a quartet of buzzers painted the color of dried blood—an eastern European, a couple, an Earl Waxen, I remember. The fourth had no name, not even a name slip. An empty apartment or someone who didn't care if he got visited. That must be Holly. I pushed the button. Somewhere in the interior of the house, a rude rattle. Not a bell, not a buzzer, a noise an angry rattlesnake with a metal tail might make. This was always the hardest part, the wait, the last rehearsal of enthusiasms.

A light flicked on in the foyer, a young girl looked through the frosted glass. A flicker of something crossed her face. But I couldn't tell what it was. Had she been waiting for someone else? Then the door opened. Holly Briggs regarded me neutrally. She wore a worn red flannel shirt; the top two buttons opened on a bony brown chest. I followed her down a narrow hallway. A large, plain-featured woman in her mid-twenties popped her head hopefully into the hall.

Holly led me into a large, cluttered room. It was a young girl's place, messy in a sort of sexy way, a mattress on the floor, clothes hanging from doors, books strewn about, a half-burnt candle beside the bed.

Outside her window a cool moon hung in the sky. "I've just run a bath," she said. "It'll have to wait now."

"Have I come too late?"

"No, this is fine," she said. "But don't stay too long. I don't know what to do with you."

There were no chairs in the room, only a thick carpet and a bed covered with a faint blue Indian bedspread. A small shaded lamp beside the bed lit the room. There was no smell of incense but I felt as if there should be. A newspaper was spread on the carpet. When Holly saw I was safely seated on the floor she allowed herself to sit on the side of the mattress. She leaned forward, shoulders rounded like an adolescent.

"You don't make jewelry here?" I asked.

"No," she said. "I sell it on commission."

"Do you make *any* of it?"

"Nope." I nodded and looked around the room. Beside the bed was an open book, face down, short stories by Isaac Bashevis Singer.

"You shouldn't leave your books like that. You'll break the spine."

She lifted the book up and closed it.

"Why are you reading him?"

She looked at the floor between her knees.

"A friend told me he was very good . . ."

"So is he?"

This was an invitation to be smart, to show off, but dismayingly she let it fall to the ground with a clatter.

"I . . . don't know."

Or the height of snobbism, I wondered. The candle beside her remained unlit.

"Look," I said, with sudden conviction, "this isn't an ad

hominem attack but you should be doing something better than selling jewelry."

"I used to know what ad hominem meant."

"It means to attack."

"Then why not say attack?" Realizing that perhaps she had been rude, she made a visible effort. "I'm trying to go back to school," she volunteered.

"I've been to school. Quite a lot," I said.

"Yes."

"So what would you study?"

"Anthropology."

Where do you go with that one? I used to have a little anthropological bit ("It's not pure coincidence, you know, that *Australopithecus africanis* had big teeth . . ."), but I hadn't had it down from the shelf in years, and I bored myself even thinking about it.

"I don't know anything about anthropology," I said.

She wrapped her arms around her knees.

"You look terribly familiar or terribly attractive, I can't tell which," I said.

"I'm not from around here."

"Do you have men coming up to you all the time in the street? You're kind of trapped there, aren't you, behind your little table. You can't very well leave. You're sort of a captive audience."

She waited for me to go on. Encouraged, I asked buoyantly: "I mean, have you ever been picked up on the street?"

"Only by the streetcar," she said flatly. "A photographer stopped me once. He said he wanted to do a big shoot with me."

"I'll bet."

"He wanted to spend fifty thousand."

I snorted.

"Yes, well," she said.

"So what happened to him?"

"I did something ugly. Eventually I always do."

I paused for a moment.

"Have *you* ever picked up anyone on the street?" I asked.

She shook her head.

"I thought not," I said.

"Although sometimes I wish I did more things . . ."

"Crossed the street more often . . ." I added.

She looked at me uncertainly to see if I meant what she did.

"Yes, I suppose."

After a moment I asked, "Did he ask you to take off your clothes?"

"No."

There was, I noticed, already a shuffle between us, a rhythm where I stepped forward and she stepped back, and I wanted it to stop before it hardened that way.

"I'm sitting on a park bench in New York. In a heavy sweater. They're in black and white," she said.

"Ah, those kind."

"Would you like to see them?"

"Not right now," I said. "Maybe in a bit," I said. I thought about asking her for one, but then I remembered the French girl on the ship and I changed my mind. I met her when I was twenty-one. She was small and dark, like a Sicilian, with bad teeth when she smiled; I never slept with her—I don't think it occurred to her—but she gave me a striking photograph of herself, all dark hair and high cheekbones. I put it in my collection of old girlfriends' photographs and sometimes a friend would pick out her picture and say wow and, loathsome as it was, if he went away thinking I'd been to bed with her, I just let it go. But it depressed me every time, like getting credit for a plagiarized paragraph, and finally I ripped it up.

"He wanted to be a Buddhist," Holly said.

"Who?"

"The photographer. He drove all the way to Los Angeles to join a commune but when he got there it was closed. So he went to the Johnny Carson Show instead."

"Is that the caliber of most of the men you meet on the street?"

"No," she said so simply that it had to be the truth.

There was a knock on the door. A woman's voice inquired, "Holly, is that your tub?"

"Just a second," Holly said.

"I just need to know," insisted the voice.

"Just a second," Holly said more firmly. I thought for an instant she was getting ready to get rid of me.

"I should let the water out of my tub," she said.

"You can have it. The tub I mean. Have it now. I can wait."

"Yes?" she said.

"Yes."

"Is it safe leaving you in here? You won't get in the bed or anything?"

"No, I won't."

"I'm very strong," she said. "I've got big muscles."

"No, Holly, I won't get in your bed."

She opened the wardrobe and removed a blue dressing gown; took a thin green towel down from a peg on the door.

"And don't answer the phone. Please."

"All right."

"It might be my mother."

"I won't do anything. I promise."

She went into the hallway and pulled the door quietly shut. I looked at her bookshelf. Unread Proust, the first volume. I wondered whom she bought that to please. No one reads Proust unless it's to fuck someone who has. A novel by Graham Greene, a paperback *Breakfast at Tiffany's*, *Leaves of Grass*, then the usual spiritual shit, Carlos Castaneda, Confucius, the *Bhagavad-Gita*, none of it read, thank God. A pair of novels by Scott Fitzgerald were almost enough to make me forgive her the two obviously read Margaret Atwood novels.

On the doorknob was a simple bracelet of dice, the faces the royalty of a pack of cards. I picked it up and looked at it. It was one of those curious objects which, when in hand, contains the ability to conjure up its owner. I remembered a kilt pin that had belonged to Georgina Buckley, my girlfriend when I was fourteen. After she dropped me, I bought a tiny bottle of her perfume, and at night I'd put it on the kilt pin and lie in bed and smell it to make her come back to me.

A box of Kleenex sat on the floor beside the bed, and it sent my imagination reeling. I saw a bare-armed Holly wiping something sticky from a man's stomach. Near the bed, the smell of her body rose up like a ghost and grabbed me by the heart. At the end of the hall I heard a door open, then close. I listened very carefully. I thought I heard a faint splash of water. I wondered if I had time.

It took longer than usual. I guess I was self-conscious. It's not how I pictured myself at forty, giving it a tug in a young girl's bedroom. I couldn't decide on the film, either. Holly in the tub, Holly standing naked beside the bed, Holly straddling me on the toilet. I didn't like that last one. Something about mixing the two functions—it seemed like, I don't know, bad taste. I flipped through the archives. Was I fucking her, was I blowing her, was she blowing me?

God, so many decisions, so little time.

Was she rubbing my cock with coconut oil?

Hmmm. A possibility.

I was still winded, my face slightly flushed, when she came back into the room. She was dressed.

"Gosh," I said, sitting up. "I almost dropped off."

She looked at the Kleenex box.

"Anyone phone?"

"Not a soul.

"You know," I said exuberantly, "I think I'm going to take off now. It's late. You're tired. I'm tired."

"Are you sure?" she said. "I'm not tired. I'm not a very good host. I don't want you to think I brought you all the way over here to wait while I had a bath."

"No no," I said, "I'm kicking myself out."

"Could you come back sometime?"

"Sure. Tomorrow."

She withdrew. "Well, tomorrow night . . ."

"Fine," I said. Fearing she'd offended me, she said quickly, "I have to work till eight-thirty. That's why I was hesitating."

I left without a handshake; no little hug as an excuse to feel her up. I hoped she noticed these niceties. She saw me down the hall. I stepped vigorously into the summer night. If there'd been a dog, I would have given him a pat. Too late, halfway down the street, I realized that I'd forgotten a piece of balled-up Kleenex under her pillow. "Christ almighty," I said to myself: it was as if a shameless madness had only just released me.

/4

I wasn't supposed to see her until eight-thirty, but I couldn't wait. I wanted to look at her. When I got close to the corner of Yonge and Bloor, I slipped into the subway, worked my way through the crowded underground passage, past fluorescent-lit Mexican food joints. The walkway teemed with shoppers and commuters; I loved the feel of it.

Tentatively, nervously, like a bridegroom wanting and not wanting to see the bride before the wedding, I climbed the stairs to street level. I stood behind the subway riders as they pushed through the revolving doors. There she was.

Flanked by a rack of flour-sack shorts, Holly looked flushed from the heat and the exhaust fumes. But there was more than that. She looked uncomfortable, exposed. She was not an outgoing girl and this job went against the grain. A bare-chested boy in a cowboy hat, a neighboring vendor, was talking to her.

She held her head slightly averted. He was standing too close to her and it made her uneasy. An antipathy for him rose up in me, hovered, and slowly died away as he moved back to his table.

She lifted a bare arm and brushed away the perspiration from her head. Under her arm, that damp, light-brown fleece. I swore, watching her out on that hot street, that I had never wanted a woman so much in my life.

She looked my way. I caught my breath and stepped back into a clutch of people. I wondered if she saw me. No sign, no recognition. I made my way back down into the subway, my head spinning. I felt like Beowulf.

How in God's name was I going to get this woman? I should take her somewhere dark and quiet. Somewhere I don't know anybody. A bar where there's no television, no baseball games, no old friends, no chatty bartenders with interesting novels behind the bar. A place where nobody, nobody, least of all my ex-wife, perish the thought, will join me.

And watch the drinking, for heaven's sake. Stay clear-headed. Don't advise her, offer to reorganize her life. And stop talking about your old girlfriends. We know you've got old girlfriends. Everyone does.

That evening, before I went to see Holly, I took my daughter Zooey out to dinner. She needed a lesson in table manners. Living with her mother, that glib noninterventionist, things had gone a little slack. Margaret was hip about manners, very *laissez-aller*. Same thing with smoking cigarettes. It was all fine, it would all take care of itself. It made me bristle with impatience.

So I took Zooey to the Other Cafe and gave her a forty-five-minute knife and fork session. Not so much as to be a bully or a pain in the ass, just enough to get the job done. When it was over, we gossiped about her mother, about a series of mysterious phone calls she'd been getting.

"She shuts herself in the bathroom," Zooey complained. "When I ask her why she's being so sneaky, she says she's not being sneaky. So I ask her what she's talking about and she says it's none of my business. You should hear her voice. She gets all excited. It really makes me mad. It's so stupid."

I walked her to the subway. I watched her make her way, with touching tentativeness, down the stairs, through the dinner crowd, stop briefly to watch a scruffy boy, her own age, light a cigarette: she was frozen with interest. Then, unaware of me, she skipped along the subway corridor on skinny colt legs.

As if shaking off a spell, I turned on my heel and hurried along the sidewalk. The sky was a disturbing grey-yellow. I ignored it. It was Saturday night and it was just beginning: couples in freshly pressed shirts, some with their hair still wet, drifted along the sidewalk. They stopped in front of restaurants; they spoke softly and then they moved on.

A red-haired woman, too old for the bright red lipstick and short black dress she wore, talked animatedly to three striking young men. "When *we* broke up he said I'd stolen the spotlight. So I said to him, 'Well, step right in!' " It was a well-practiced story, and the young men all laughed.

In apartment windows, children sat overlooking the street. Headlights came on. A taxi dragged slowly by, meter up, hood light on.

A sharp-featured boy, an Asian in a flowered blue shirt, walked by in tight black pants, a pack of cigarettes in his hand. He didn't want to spoil the line of his trousers.

Weary fathers walked ahead of their wives and children. In

the window of the Corona Restaurant, a pretty blond girl with a sharp nose sat alone. At the next table, an older man, fortyish, in a black leather jacket, also alone, watched her.

A stocky man wearing gym shorts and a muscle T-shirt listened to a Walkman as he strode home.

A drunk picked his way along the sidewalk, stepping stiff-legged like a syphilitic.

Two gay men emerged from a side street. Their conversation had a kind of charged enthusiasm—they were on a first date, and it was going well. I envied them.

A clutch of young men in gleaming whites headed for a beer-swilling, table-banging, wet-T-shirt night at the Brunswick Tavern.

This was the best part of Saturday night, when everything was just about to begin, everything was still possible.

Bloor Street twinkled in soft summer light and girls moved along the sidewalk in summer pastels and ineffable perfumes.

A prematurely yellowed leaf dropped from a tree above the Other Cafe. A mustached man reading a novel looked up and with some amusement picked up the leaf and put it between the pages of his book.

A couple of plainclothes cops walked by. "If you treat your wife like shit, she's gonna jump someone," one said. His companion nodded numbly and stared straight ahead.

"Which is what happened," he said.

I wanted to get ready for Holly. So I went to the gym. On a Saturday night, I had it to myself, a big gleaming, echoing cave. I ran around and around a green putty track; I ran until my face got hot and my hair matted with sweat at the back of my neck. I took a shower; I dried my hair under a hand dryer; at one point I snapped my head around to see if anyone was sneaking up on me. I walked out past row after row of dark green lockers. I felt pure-skinned as soapstone.

Under a light-blue sky, I drifted along the sidewalk. At an outdoor cafe, a crowded table of heavyset European men, jittery from too many cigarettes and too much *café noir*, tapped their feet with boredom and fell silent. I felt sorry for them, sorry for anyone who wasn't coming with me tonight. I couldn't understand how I got through all those other nights in my life without this to look forward to.

Green-eyed Holly Briggs lingered behind her table, awkwardly, like an adolescent boy at the edge of a party. I detected a trace of eyeliner, even perfume, very faint. She wore a murderous bloodred turtleneck that sucked the color from her cheeks.

We drifted down through quiet summer streets, past blue-hued windows where young men watched television, down through Chinatown. Darkness swallowed the last turquoise patch of sky. I talked. Holly listened.

I was very keyed up and showing off like mad. I made astute connections; I threw similes into the summer air like brightly colored balls. But I wondered if any of it was registering. I had a vague feeling that none of it mattered, not enough, that none of it was going below her neck. I wondered whether she was even aware of me on that level. I was certainly the smartest man she'd met, I implied that several times, but there was no tension on her part, no self-consciousness, no effort, none of the goodies that come at you when a woman wants you. She seemed not to care if I thought her bright or different; she wasn't trying. And that made her drop-dead sexy.

"I'm talking too much," I said.

Carried along by the crowd, we moved down Spadina, along Front Street, through the revolving doors of the cavernous train station. On a Saturday night, it had a kind of spectacular loneliness. I've always had the suspicion that I'm going to finish my days in a place like that, a high-ceilinged, drafty way station, waiting for a bus or a train to take me somewhere profoundly irrelevant.

We came out the side doors. I suggested we peek into a wine bar across the park. I hadn't been there for years, not since I was barred. We crossed a shadowy wedge of lawn and plunged down a steep set of stairs. Inside it was teeming. The opera had just got out; women in hallucinatorily vivid makeup and tuxedoed gentlemen drank red wine and made bright observations. It smelt like my parents' parties.

"We're not dressed for this," Holly said, shrinking.

"Do you give a fuck?" I whispered. It sounded very good, very naughty amid the diamond rings and cigar smoke. I tried to take her hand but she kept it obdurately in her windbreaker pocket.

"Yes," she said.

The bartender from the old days (the one whose tomato plants I had ripped up in a drunken, demented rage several months after he bruised my collar bone) was now the manager. He was balding; under strings of curly black hair his scalp shone onion-white. I had a fleeting, private realization that our young bodies were gone, that nothing would ever bring them back. No diet, no tan, no jogging; they were simply gone forever.

He recognized me instantly and shook his head with amused weariness, led us to a table, dropped two menus crisply in front of us and disappeared. It wasn't until I was seated that I realized my palms were perspiring.

At the far end of the room, a man with a big handsome head and immaculate clothes leaned rather awkwardly on the bar. He was my age, perhaps a few years older; there was a starchy, tense formality about him. He was talking to a wide-shouldered woman bartender, a real Amazon. She refilled his glass with white wine. I had the idle thought that they were sleeping together.

He cast a look our way and resumed his conversation. Then I forgot about him. I was trying to get Holly to talk about herself. She was embarrassed, I think, about the flatness of her life and in her resignation to it, there was a casual, deep-set unhappiness. Unlike me, she had no fascination with her past, with the poetic miracle that led her to "here."

She'd grown up in a nondescript little town on the shore of Lake Ontario, the daughter of a small-town newspaper editor who'd finished his days paving driveways. He drank a bit. Her mother was still alive, still lived in one of those towns whose name alone fills you with a strange ennui, the boredom of quiet parlors and sunlight on wood floors.

She failed grade nine, said it was a lark, which it obviously wasn't because her self-esteem was still quietly reeling from it. I don't know anyone who's failed a grade in school who hasn't been, to some degree, untouchably wounded by it. She got a driver's license the day she was sixteen, "to get out of town," had her first boyfriend that fall. "He just wore me down," she said, but didn't elaborate. That same year she left school, thereby disqualifying herself from university. It was a decision she now regretted. "I keep planning to do a make-up year," she said, "but I just don't seem to be able to make it all the way downtown to pick up the application forms." Her weariness, feigned or real, I didn't know then, disguised a tremendous disappointment and I wanted desperately to make her happy, I was sure I could, that I'd just love her enough and make her bad luck go away. Because, peculiar as it may sound, I was lucky. I'd known for years that virtually all my suffering was luxurious, self-induced. If I wanted to be happy, all I had to do was go a couple of days without a hangover.

At the age of nineteen Holly Briggs moved to Toronto; she got an apartment, bang, like that, on Melrose Avenue and then, bang, like that got a job in a film-production company. Things looked very good for a while. "I got the job with wet hair," she said. It was a curious triumph for her, something she was proud of, and her vanity awoke briefly from its slumber. But then small-town luck caught up with her, things stopped happening unbidden, and the film company folded.

"I haven't been up to much since then," she said with a little laugh. "That's about it. Honest."

"Really?" I said, locked forward in my chair as if catching lilacs at the foot of Buddha.

Out of the corner of my eye, I noticed a flourish of movement out of pace with the rest of the room. The wine drinker, the handsome one at the bar, put down his glass decisively and swept over to our table. He looked very angry.

Holly looked up.

"Hello, Jonathan," she said, with carefully modulated surprise.

"I wish you wouldn't come here," he burst out rashly. "I rather enjoy this place."

I was stunned. Before either of us could respond, he whirled around and rushed heavily from the bar, his perfectly pressed raincoat flying behind him.

I looked at Holly in some amazement, glad, in some cretinous way, to be privy, to be on her side of this bizarre encounter. It should have pulled us a notch closer, but Holly appeared to resent my curiosity.

"Well," I said brightly, "You've been up to something, that's for sure."

She didn't respond. I looked at the door through which the angry man had just fled. Of course they were fucking, I knew that. Or had been. A tiff between friends, no matter how grave, can't generate that kind of shaking rage. But I also noted, with some relief, that it sounded over between them. His unhappy outburst had had a nothing-to-lose thrust. That understood, I welcomed a new subject to be smart about. I'm very strong on embittered boyfriends. But Holly wouldn't play ball. What seemed like guarded privacy wasn't. She had, in fact, so little interest in him, in their time together, that she seemed barely able to summon up the energy to talk about it.

I found this scary, to be honest. I prodded her gently. I've been around long enough to know that how the last guy got treated is probably how you're going to get treated. Finally out it came. "We had a little fling," she said. "It wasn't even a fling. It was a flingette. I slept with him a half-dozen times. I knew it wasn't a good idea but I had a whole lot of stuff that was making me very unhappy and I thought it might make me feel better. But it didn't, of course. It never does. Does it?"

"Go on," I said. I ordered another drink. Two of them, in fact, eight-ounce glasses of Piesporter something. It cost a fortune but right then I didn't give a fuck. The conversation was giving me a ferocious thirst, not to mention heartburn. I had a kind of frozen smile on my face. I didn't know how I was supposed to look about the idea of someone else sleeping with her, when I hadn't yet.

"Go on," I said again, stonily, when the wine arrived. "Tell me."

So she did, God help me.

"He's very kind, reads a lot. We just weren't very sympatico."
She seemed to take an inward start. "It just works with some
people. And it didn't with us. No one's fault." She stopped,
uncomfortable.

"I was just curious," I said. I knew I looked driven and hot
eyed. "Go on."

"Well, that's it. I got drunk one night and I went over to
his apartment and told him I couldn't do it anymore." She
paused. I followed behind her, right over the cliff.

"Did you fuck him?"

She nodded and raised her eyebrows. I felt a stab of pain
like a fresh betrayal. My mouth went dry. For once in my life
I was without comment.

She went on. "For a couple of months, he wandered around
my neighborhood like a ghost trying to run into me. I used
to watch him through the front window. He dropped in once,
some guy was there, I forget who. Jonathan was drunk, he'd
been drinking red wine and it makes him very . . ." she looked
for the right word—"volatile." She smiled. I couldn't look at
her enough. It killed me when she smiled like that. I thought
my life would be a sham, a second best if I didn't get to make
love to her, if only once.

"He flew off the handle about God knows what and crashed
out of the apartment. The guy was terrified. But he came back
twenty minutes later, all formal and dignified, and then he
took us both out to a bar, me *and* the guy, and bought us a
very expensive bottle of wine."

"So . . ." I was looking for a tactful phrase but Holly an-
ticipated it.

"I sent the guy home in a taxi with him."

I looked at her carefully, surprised.

"I just couldn't leave Jonathan on the street with that imagination of his."

He was waiting for us in the park shadows as we left the bar.

"What am I supposed to do?" I whispered as he came swiftly toward us. I hoped nothing. He was stocky, considerably stronger than I. Up close he looked Slavic, which is to say repressed and explosive, and the sheer power of his feelings intimidated me. He was like a kettle with its top welded shut. I imagined him capable of real violence.

"I apologize, I'm terribly sorry," he said rather stiffly to Holly.

I moved off down the sidewalk. They went into the park. After perhaps five minutes, they emerged from the darkness. She was talking. He nodded his head with slightly exaggerated attention. He seemed mollified, his vibrating tension eased.

He shook my hand. I nodded.

"It's all right now," he said. "We've recontacted, that's the important thing."

He turned to her. "Then I'll see you about?"

"Good night, Jonathan."

He shook my hand again, nodded curtly and moved off down the sidewalk, a haunted man in a beautiful raincoat. I felt a pang of terrific sadness for him.

Then I realized I was watching myself, six weeks, six months, down the road.

It was well after midnight when we turned up Holly's leafy street. Bloor Street still buzzed with light and activity. Exuberant students burst from bars and ran into traffic. The outdoor cafes were full. A white boy strummed a guitar and shrieked "Not Fade Away" on the corner. A drunken girl picked a flower from a flower box in front of the ice cream shop. But as we moved up Melrose Avenue, the sounds—the guitar, the excited summer voices, the traffic—dimmed. There was that smell again, salty, raunchy. It enveloped us in a bell.

A bicycle ticked down the street. We walked on in silence. The houses were tall, darkened. We stepped into pools of yellow light, our shadows racing to catch up, then sprinting quickly ahead. The moon showed itself between sharp gables. Sweat trickled down the inside of my arm. We had run out of things to say. I had talked myself hoarse. Holly was tired, I sensed. She wanted me not to talk. The trees arched, almost touching overhead. An air conditioner hummed from an upper story. Twenty yards ahead was a tree, a thick-trunked tree illuminated at the base. I'll wait till I get there, I thought, then I'll ask her. When I get opposite that tree, I'll ask her. And then the tree was behind me, and I was light-headed with dread.

"Holly," I said. "Do you think it would be the worst idea in the world if I stayed the night?" It came out in a torrent, like one word.

At first I thought she hadn't heard me. She walked on in silence and then crossed the street. I followed a step behind. We were almost at the house. I could see her bicycle on the porch.

"Sure," she said. "Why not."

Inside the apartment, she opened the window and pulled the curtains. "Just a minute," she said, and went into the bathroom.

I sat on the edge of the bed. I couldn't remember what to do. What was good manners. I turned off the overhead light and lit a candle. No, that was presumptuous. I blew out the candle; turned the light back on. But I didn't want to risk a forced and unnatural kiss that might make her change her mind. Better presumptuous than inept, I decided. I lit the candle again, turned off the light and sprang into bed, leaving my clothes folded on the chair like a good schoolboy. The bathroom door opened. She gave a little start.

"Oh," she said. She got into bed. I could smell toothpaste. She was wearing a blue dressing gown. I waited for a minute, then five. Then she asked simply: "Do you snore?"

"No," I said.

I waited for her to take off the dressing gown.

"Maybe we should just do it and get it over with," she said.

I propped myself up on my hand.

"Holly," I said. I looked at her breasts under the dressing gown. "Is that all you under there?"

She didn't answer.

At four o'clock in the morning I pulled her gently toward me. She was very warm. I parted her dressing gown.

"Don't come inside me," she said.

/5

*I*n the blue morning light, Holly Briggs slept on her back, an arm thrown over her head. Her underwear lay on the carpet. Under the covers it smelt like sex. It must have been seven-thirty, maybe eight o'clock. I eased out of bed. I wanted to steal out of the apartment, go off someplace alone. Like a miser counting his money, I wanted to shut myself up in a room and go over the evening, word by word, gesture by gesture. Holly rolled over, her back to me. It was a sign, I thought, a sign that we should leave it like this. I tiptoed by her bed and into the bathroom. I picked a bloodred toothbrush from the stand and ran my thumb along the bristles. A fine, faint cool mist. Even it gave off a sexual charge. I turned on the tap very softly. I looked at myself in the mirror. I went back into the dark bedroom, picked my pants off the floor, put on my shirt, scribbled a note in black eyeliner on the newspaper and leaned it against the mirror.

Then I stepped outside.

The street lay in cool, green shadows.

I could smell bacon frying somewhere. Birds shrieked in the trees overhead. Behind the Catholic girls' school, a white, waxy sun rose in the blue sky. Bars of light stretched across the street and spread across the red brick face of Holly's house.

A clutch of schoolgirls in black and white tunics came up the street; they had children's knees, and it robbed them of their sexiness. The street smelled warm, it smelled of grass and dogs. I rubbed my nose. My hand smelled of Holly. Thinking of her lying under the sheet made my stomach sink. I looked up the street. I couldn't see her house now; it was obscured by a maple tree. I smelled my hand again. I started slowly back up the street. I could hear the change jingle in my pockets. Holly's driveway was splashed in sunlight. Water drops glistened like diamonds on the seat of her bicycle. I reached very slowly for the doorknob. I stepped into the blue shadows.

Holly was sound asleep. I took off my shirt and lowered my pants to the floor before I heard a sheet rustle.

"I forgot to tell you something," I said. I lowered myself onto the bed and pulled the sheet back. I kissed her once, lightly, right where her leg met her body.

"I can't come in the morning," she said, raising my head up; she said it sleepily, sweetly. "Come here." I held her wrist, very lightly, over her head. I touched my lips under her arm. I slipped into her body; I didn't move, I didn't have a chance to. She looked right at me, expressionless, and I came. A dead faintness followed, as if I were going to pass out, and then the skin on my arms was washed in a wave of goosebumps.

She watched me silently as I got dressed again.

"Now you're probably wondering what all the fuss was about," she said.

I kissed her on the lips.

"Maybe you better wash your face before you go," she said.

"No," I said.

The porch was drenched in divine sunlight. A prop-driven plane flew overhead. I stopped a beautiful girl in a white dress to ask the time. She was suspicious, naturally, but my sheer good spirits, the volume of my enthusiasm disarmed her and we walked a block together before I gave her a cheery good-bye and moved on. She looked surprised, even a little disappointed.

It was as if the world had been given a spanking new coat of paint.

I walked down that street, my body humming.

The red flowers in the garden across the street reminded me of the roses in the flower boxes in Mexico; the dark, damp patios smelled of summer holidays when I was a little boy, of lying stomach-down on the dock and fishing for sunfish.

The wind picked up. It rushed through the thick leaves. Somewhere, a bell rang. I followed along a line of silent parked cars until I got to the foot of Melrose Avenue. The Indians slept in the park. Across the street, in the Other Cafe, I spotted Spolin. He was bent over a notebook. I was tempted to call out to him, but something told me that once I stopped, once I spoke to someone, the spell would be broken. So I turned east and kept walking.

I was hungry, famished in fact, but I didn't want to stop. The street was streaked with vivid colors, green shorts, brown legs, glaring white running shoes. Words, shreds of music, memories streamed like honey: I wanted to pause to write them down, but I knew better. I knew that would make the magic stop.

It was almost more than I could stand. I wanted to do something, douse it down, eat something, phone someone, have a drink . . . It occurred to me that happiness was a physical sensation, almost an uncomfortable one.

At the corner of Yonge and Bloor a short, bundled-up woman with the face of a crab apple cursed at the traffic. Across the street under the dazzling sunlight the street vendors formed an island on the opposite corner, T-shirts flying like flags.

Holly wasn't there today. Holly was home in bed.

I passed by a collectors' record store. The Beatles burst forth cheerily. They sounded smaller, more simplistic than I remembered. I wondered if I'd outgrown them at last.

I could feel a small headache starting in my right temple. I looked at my watch. It was noon. I wandered on a few more steps, then I stopped. Something had changed. Somewhere in the last block it had just slipped away. The spell was over. Sweetly over, but over. I was back in my life again. I was famished.

/6

*T*hat summer, rain seemed like something that happened in a foreign country.

A couple of nights later, I woke up at two-thirty in the morning. I was covered in sweat, my hand between my legs. I was frantic for her. I knew I'd come to die. I went down the stairs. The glass door clattered behind me. One night it was going to fall from its socket like an eye. I hurried up through the hot streets. The world sweated sex. I was in such a hurry I would have stepped over the body of my mother. I could hear myself breathing. I felt haunted, like I was setting off for a murder. I hurried down her alleyway, my heart banging. I was afraid. I braced myself to see something terrible. I looked through the glass. But there was only a lump under the sheet. I tried the window. It was locked. When Holly slept alone, she locked the window. On nights like this, she'd dream and sweat in an airless room. I could see the reflection of the moon in the glass. The sheet stirred, a body appeared to float upright and swim toward me. Bare-armed Holly materialized in the glass. She opened the window; she went back to bed. I hiked myself into the room.

I put my hand under the sheet. Her skin was damp. "I was dreaming about the Shah of Iran," she said. "God, I've got a headache."

I brushed her hair off her forehead.

"I should have a shower," she said.

"No, please don't."

"I should brush my teeth at least."

I kissed her mouth. Her lips were dry and warm.

"You taste lovely."

She swallowed.

"I thought there might be someone here," I said.

She went still. She rested a sleepy hand on my face. I could tell her eyes were closed.

"If you get me a glass of water . . ." she said, then seemed to drift off again. A moment later: "Is that why you came over?"

"No."

She reached down and touched me. She laughed sleepily.

"That's why you came."

She put her arms behind her head. I could feel myself coming apart.

"Let me give you a blow job," I said.

"Men don't give women blow jobs."

"Whatever it's called."

"Whatever it's called," she repeated sleepily. "Are all forty-year-olds this keen?"

I pulled back the sheet. She tasted salty.

"Are you counting backwards?"

"No," I said.

"Do you really like doing that?"

"Yes."

"Do I taste all right?"

"Lovely."

She lifted my hand from her waist and put it on her breast.

My neck started to hurt; it made that funny silent cracking noise. I slid down the mattress until my knees touched the carpeted floor. I reached up and took her under the knees and pulled her down the mattress.

"Don't," she said.

I put my tongue on her again. Don't think about making her come, I reminded myself. Just taste her, smell her, think about nothing else. A Zen blow job, as it were. When her breathing came faster I ignored it. I maintained the same pace, like a robot tennis player. Indefatigable. Don't aim for the finish line. In a Zen blow job, there is no finish line.

She breathed in quickly, three times. Then silence. It didn't come, it was fading. She was chasing it.

"Don't hurry," I said.

"Aren't you getting tired?" she asked anxiously.

"I love doing it," I said.

"You don't get tired?"

"No, never."

"Really?"

"Really."

I put a finger inside her and put it in my mouth. She looked down at me, surprised.

"I wish I could keep you on my hands all day," I said.

She closed her eyes. She put her hands on the sides of my head.

"Is this why boys have ears?"

I started again. She tiptoed up the side of the mountain; she tiptoed right to the edge; she peeked over and again she grew self-conscious. But I didn't stop, I didn't tire, I didn't change rhythm and suddenly she breathed in quickly, one, two, three times, half sat up and came. I looked right at her. She looked away; it was a reflex. She didn't want me to see her like that.

She lay back down, her arm over her eyes.

I sat up on my haunches. A drop passed right through me, clear as a rain drop, and fell onto my leg. Another drop appeared. I caught it on my finger.

"Look what you do to me," I said and very softly rubbed it on her lower lip. Motionless, she looked at me. I touched myself again but she stopped my hand and began on me awkwardly with her own.

"Why won't you put your mouth on me?" I asked.

"I'm shy," she said. I took her hand away.

"I want to," she said.

A few pumps with that tanned hand and I came on the sheets; she moved her head back.

In the next couple of weeks, I took Holly Briggs to all my favorite places, and it never occurred to me I might be poisoning half the city for myself; that after she was gone, the place might be uninhabitable. One afternoon, I stopped by her vending table; just looking at her drove me into such a frenzy I begged her to "have a coffee" with me. I led her by the hand into Carlevale's, a glassed-in coffee shop nearby. A couple of days before I'd noticed that the men's washroom, a single compartment with a lock on the door, was marked OUT

OF ORDER. I took her in there, bent her over the toilet bowl and blasted away at her, not until I came, but until my legs gave out. Holly was a short girl and after crouching a while, my legs locked in a fiery cramp. Anyway, the point is I can't use that bathroom anymore without thinking about her. Same goes for a lot of places around here.

We rocketed up the side of the CN Tower in a glass bubble elevator, the city spread below us like a sea of anemones. We sat in silence.

"After ten minutes, it's no different than watching television," she said.

I can't go by the CN Tower now without remembering that.

We took a bus tour around the city. We went for a midnight stroll through my old high school. The ghosts of young boys lingered like prostitutes in the cool, green hallways.

Sometimes, I had the suspicion that Holly was looking for someone. That I was just keeping her company. I wanted her so much I could never tell if it was intuition or paranoia. Perhaps she was seeking out the dark-haired man, hoping for a glimpse, hoping for him to see her with me. Sometimes, I confess, I nursed a wish that she'd go out and do something terrible, go out and fuck him and tell me. Get it over with, just so I could know what I was up against. I felt like one of those poor sea lions that get so scared they jump right into the jaws of a killer whale: like me, they just can't stand suspense. I mean, if someone holds a gun to your head, you sort of wish they'd go ahead and pull the trigger.

And then other times, when I was inside her, I wanted to beg her never to be with anyone else, because it'd kill me if she did.

It wouldn't, of course.

And it didn't.

But sometimes just the idea made me feel as if I were going off my rocker.

One afternoon, for example, I was having lunch by myself in the Other Cafe. I overheard a conversation between two young women; a dark-haired girl in her twenties, the prettier of the two, was talking guardedly about a love affair that had just ended. The man, I gathered, lived in another city, three hundred miles away. For the better part of a year she had shuttled back and forth on weekends, the understanding being that when he tied up some things, he would join her in Toronto. After a while she began to have the uncomfortable feeling that he was quite happy with things the way they were, that they could go on like this forever. She found his casual inertia alarming. Recently she'd discovered that he had renewed the lease on his apartment; he had left the document lying around. So, very abruptly, she ended things.

Her friend, who had been listening rapturously, interjected. "But the passion," she insisted, "it must have been great: imagine traveling three hundred miles every weekend just to get laid."

"Perhaps," her friend agreed cautiously, with the control of someone who is trying to convince herself of something. "But you know, I think maybe passion is just a response to having something you're not supposed to have."

Well, that made me put my fork down.

God, what a concept. And from one so tender in years. No, I said, that can't be it.

But it stayed with me all afternoon.

Later that day, it was a Sunday, Holly sunned herself on the wooden patio in back of her house. The sun poured down honey-hot. I watched her from the doorway. She wore white underwear, with J-O-C-K-E-Y in small gold letters across the elastic. Holly had that curious, slightly oily skin that, after only a splash of sun, tans like buttered mahogany, and she was looking devastatingly good. But I'd already fucked her in the morning, so I was sort of honor bound to go to the back of the line. She poured a handful of coconut oil and rubbed it slowly on her legs, her calves, the base of her neck. Then she dabbed her cheekbones and cleaned the oil from between her fingers. Childrens' voices floated over the rosebush. A flying ant wandered across the grey patio, wings out, and disappeared down a crack.

In the next yard, a plain dress hung motionless on the clothesline.

A conch shell, faded and peeling, lay on the corner of the deck.

"Where'd you get that?" I asked.

"From a friend," she said. The shell took on an exotic, threatening hue. I picked it up and put it to my ear. A single key—Holly's spare house key, I guessed, lay beneath it.

"Nothing," I said.

"What?"

"You're supposed to hear the sea," I said. "But I guess this one's a clunker." She lay back, her eyes closed. She brushed away a fly. On her arm, a white vaccination mark. It belonged to a part of her life I had never witnessed, when I didn't exist, and that made it sexy.

The sun blinked, a shade fell. Then the clouds passed and the eye opened, the heat swelled. A sea gull soared low over the roofs, looking for something.

Holly was preoccupied. Her brow wrinkled in a frown. Her answers were curt, friendly but final. I wondered if she was thinking about the black-haired man. Did she miss him? Why did she never mention him?

The frown deepened.

"It'll give you lines," I said.

"What?"

"Frowning."

She grunted and returned to her train of thought. She scratched her stomach with a ringed finger and turned her head quickly to the side, as if she were pushing away a thought.

She's thinking she'll never make love to him again, I thought.

She put her arms behind her head. Like a restless sleeper she could not stay still.

Her skin glistened with coconut oil. A towel lay draped over her breasts. For some reason, that set off an alarm bell. I couldn't figure out why. Then I remembered. Years before, in the Caribbean, I'd known an American woman who loved going topless. She simply wouldn't or couldn't keep her tits under wraps—except when she went in the sun. Then she covered up. It turned out her boyfriend liked her tits white.

"He likes to put his dinky there," she told an astonished couple from Alberta.

I wondered if Holly was keeping her tits white for someone. I wanted to ask her but I couldn't find words that wouldn't, to some degree, reduce my stature in her eyes.

I found myself wondering what Margaret would do. There were no sacred cows with her, only preciousness. Margaret would come right out and say it. Holly, are you keeping your tits white for someone?

"Holly," I said, and I made it to the end of the sentence before I lost my nerve, before my voice betrayed a telltale waver. But just saying the words shattered their spell. I don't remember her answer; I had already moved onto something else.

But as my ex-wife says, once the green snake is out of the bag, it's a bitch to get it back in again. There was another episode.

Spolin came with Holly and me to see *Dirty Harry* at a repertory theater out near High Park. I once met a Brit on a Channel ferry who said it was the only movie he'd cross London on a rainy night to see, and I agree with him. I'd seen it six times already. But during the film my imagination started to run away with me. I confess at one point I looked over discreetly to see if Holly and Spolin were holding hands. They weren't. But he did put his hand in her popcorn box, a gesture that struck me, struck my poisoned heart that is, as, I don't know, provocatively familiar. She left her box on her lap and he dug his hand in. You see what I mean.

Afterwards, we wandered along the street, Holly and Spolin lagging slightly behind, talking. Neither liked the film. "Childish," Spolin said. He was pissed off at me for not phoning him for three weeks: Spolin was a little bit like an old girlfriend that way. Eager to detect slights, he kept careful track of who called whom. Holly agreed silently.

Their rapport rankled me. It seemed to suggest tacitly that they agreed there was something vaguely wrong with me, with anyone who liked the film as much as I did. I made a mental note never, ever to see Spolin again in Holly's company. I know I was behaving like a teenager, I knew it at the time, but that's the thing about the green snake, you can't do anything about it.

I fell into a miserable silence. To make things worse, the counter girl at the cinema had put butter on my popcorn and so, having gobbled it down, I felt greasy and unattractive, as if my stomach was hanging over my belt and unpleasant growths were sprouting on my back.

Now Spolin is a needle-nosed fellow whom some women find very attractive; he's also rather short, and eight or nine years younger than I. You can see where this is going. The fact that it's a headache-inducing cliché made me all the grumpier. Somehow, they looked like a nice young couple in the company of a large-faced buffoon, grinning foolishly in an attempt to keep the attention of the young girl who, for some (doubtless pathological) reason, was letting him diddle her. For now. Until something better came along. Which, at this very moment, it might just be.

At one point, I crossed the sidewalk and went into a brightly lit tobacco store to buy something, I can't remember what. Perhaps nothing at all. Perhaps merely to see who would follow me. Holly remained on the sidewalk with Spolin. I watched them through the window. She asked questions, watched him intently while he spoke. Spolin, warming to his audience, self-conscious under her gaze, put his hands in his jacket pockets and grazed one foot back and forth over a patch of pavement in front of him as if he were brushing it clear. I'd seen him do it before. It was pretend-thoughtful. He did it when he knew he was doing well.

I joined them on the sidewalk.

I stared glassily at the street.

"God I'm tired," I said. "Maybe you two should keep on. I'm going home."

I was committing suicide and Spolin sensed it.

He shook his head wearily. "I'm beat," he said. I half expected him to yawn and stretch. "Besides, my mother's coming at the crack of dawn to clean my apartment."

Holly laughed.

"Your mother cleans your apartment?"

"Pays the rent too," he said. "I'm an underachiever."

When he turned down his street a block later, I was relieved. He was doing far too well.

7

"*I* bought you a present," I said. I picked the package off the floor. She opened it. It was a long-sleeved, dark green shirt. When I think of Holly sitting up in bed with that green shirt half open, it makes me dizzy. Still. I don't think I'll ever get it out of my head.

I lay on the bed, talking. She was looking at me but, like a bad interviewer, her eyes were not there; she was thinking about something else. Suddenly she interrupted me.

"I have to go out tomorrow night," she said softly. "It's a birthday party."

After a lingering moment I asked, "Whose birthday, Holly?"

"You know whose birthday."

I felt stricken.

"His mother is throwing a birthday party for him. *She* invited me. I have to go." I lay on my back. I was having trouble breathing. Even more trouble not showing it.

"Bix, I can see a vein beating in your throat. I don't want you to have a fit about this."

"I have a poisoned heart," I said gloomily and rolled over on my back. "This is God punishing me."

"Does he punish you often?"

"He's a busy guy but he finds time."

"Has he spoken to you about this birthday party?"

I shook my head.

"Perhaps God's not interested in birthdays."

"Perhaps not."

I was waiting for her to volunteer something, to see me after the party, but she didn't. And I suspected it was deliberate.

As if reading my thoughts, she said, "You don't want another wife, do you?"

"Are you going to sleep with him?"

"No."

I couldn't stop my heart bucking. I wanted to gasp for air. I tried to make a joke.

"What if he wants to? What if he rubs up against you at the party?"

"I'll jerk him off. No big deal."

That made me sick.

"I'm joking," she said.

She sat up in bed.

"If I show you my tits, will you stop sulking?"

"I don't think I can do anything."

Eight minutes later I was begging her to suck my cock and make me come.

But she didn't. She wouldn't take my cock in her mouth. I thought back to an old girlfriend, a goony actress who'd do everything but kiss me. Everybody, I guess, holds on to something.

By noon the next day, I was back at my table at the Other Cafe, looking out on the street. It hadn't hit me yet. My body was still humming from Holly. I thought it was fine, do-able, manageable, understandable. A birthday party, a night for old times' sake with an old boyfriend. Big deal. Like she said.

Later, at my kitchen table, I dawdled with a speech on catastrophe insurance (we were for it). As it got dark, couples drifted along the street under the eternal electronic smile of the booby hatch. I got tired, and the devils crept in. The sunlight retreated, something stirred in my stomach. I looked at my watch. It was eight-thirty. I imagined the birthday party, a lavish affair. Lavish but not intimate. Something Scott Fitzgerald might have liked. Scott was, after all, a man who enjoyed a good party. Plenty of people and noisy talk. Plenty of light. A comforting thought. "Anyway," as Holly said, "his mother is going to be there. Nothing can happen at a party with your mother in the room."

Outside my apartment, the Chinaman toiled in his garden. I went for a walk. Or what I thought was a walk. In fact I made a beeline for the Other Cafe. I looked at my watch again. By now they would be opening the presents. What did Holly buy for him? A shirt? A watch? He already had a watch. Did she wear the green shirt to the party? I hoped she wore a bra with it.

I came to a crashing halt in the middle of the sidewalk. In one stomach-plunging second, I realized I had made a dreadful omission. I had asked her if she was going to fuck him, but not whether she was going to stay the night. Or had I? No, I hadn't. If she wasn't going to fuck him, it didn't matter if she spent the night.

Yes, but, if she spent the night, maybe she'd fuck him. Maybe he'd rub up against her in the night. What would she do then? Jerk him off. So that's what she meant. She must have known she was going to spend the night.

Would she wear the shirt to bed? Would she take it off in the bathroom? Would he unbutton it? Would he start with the bottom button or the top? What would those sea-green eyes look at while he unbuttoned her shirt?

I ordered a martini.

No, my shirt, my green shirt would protect her like a wreath of garlic.

But I couldn't stop myself: I saw the green shirt lying like a dark stain on the carpet at the foot of the bed. Grey dawn light seeped under the curtain; it stirred in the breeze. Outside on the street, a car started up, the driver raced the engine and Holly rolled onto her back, her arm thrown over her head.

A brown body, narrow-chested, slumbered beside her.

It was his apartment. I strained to see. A chest of drawers, tall, dark-brown, like his chest. The window was open and the room was cool, awash in a graceful breeze.

Jesus. Enough.

Right now, Holly was at the party. What were those green eyes looking at? What was that mouth saying? That mouth. Why won't she suck my cock?

I called the waitress. "Vodka martini," I said.

Then I remembered that I don't like the finality of a lone martini, the inevitable "Well, what now?" it seems to raise. With a martini, you need to know there's a future, that there's somewhere to go afterwards.

I called the waitress back. It must have sounded urgent. The couple at the next table looked over. The golden bottle of wine chilling in a bucket united them. The waitress, amused, came back.

"I'd like an imported beer with that," I said with eager, schoolboy politeness.

The couple resumed a low-tide murmur.

"What kind of imported beer?" She was humoring me. For one ghastly second I suspected she knew everything.

"Something in a green bottle."

The martini arrived in a tulip-shaped glass, frosted, with a twist of lemon. I pulled out the lemon rind with my fingers and dropped it in the ashtray. I didn't want it getting in the way. I drank the martini in three short gulps. It made my eyes water.

The beer arrived. I was right: just its presence reassured me.

Surely she wouldn't wear my shirt.

The upward spreading warmth of the martini bled across my face and I gazed out the window. Thank God for martinis. They stop the poisoned mind dead in its tracks. I smiled with patronizing amusement at the notion of my having a poisoned mind. Perhaps it is the function of a poisoned mind to analyze itself as poisoned. No matter. The implications left me slightly vertiginous.

Let the snakes rattle in the can; just don't let them out.

But why are there snakes in the can?

Doesn't matter. Let them rattle.

Yes, but what if she spends the night?

She'd only do it to be polite.

Someone in the restaurant guffawed.

Perhaps she'll turn up here. Perhaps I should phone the party. Let her know I'm here. Just in case.

No. Too transparent, too sweaty-palmed. You couldn't fool a camel with a ruse like that.

I smiled indulgently.

No. It's his birthday, I reasoned, floating on a martini wave, don't spoil it for him.

A pretty girl in summer shorts and a dark ponytail stopped her bicycle in front of the cafe window. Indeed the world was full of women to be loved. If something happened with Holly, there would be others. There always were, there always had been.

Another guffaw from across the restaurant. I looked over, irritated. A thick bespectacled fat man stuffed a forkful of linguini into his maw and chewed it with his mouth open. You could see it falling from the roof of his mouth, like laundry in a dryer. I wanted to smack him.

I poured the beer into a glass. I'd have to drink it soon. It was getting warm. Another problem.

I went downstairs to the bathroom; stopped at the urinal, stared blankly down at the cold, white porcelain. If she stays the night, she'll fuck him. And if she fucks him, she'll probably suck his cock, en route. Just to be polite. I gazed miserably at the graffiti in front of my face. I zipped up, turned around and looked in the mirror. I was alone.

"Did you stay the night?" I asked the mirror. "You did?"

Too tentative. I tried again.

"Did you stay the night?" I raised my eyebrows. "You did." I shrugged. It was going well. "Sorry, it's over."

No, I didn't like that "over" business. Made you sound childish.

I started again. When I got to the trouble spot, I improvised. "Let's just leave it for a while." *Then* the shrug. Much better. More European. Worldly. Lacks that peevish flavor. It also left the future open. You don't want to slam the door on your own fingers. I mean, once you give her the axe, what then?

I looked again into the mirror. Something was making me feel very sick. Surely I was missing the point.

"God Holly, how could you have done that?" My voice wavered.

"It was no big deal," she answered.

"Your casualness terrifies me." My face darkened in the mirror.

A man emerged from a toilet stall and went quickly out the door.

I stared in the mirror. I shook my head.

Then I went back upstairs, taking the stairs two at a time. My table was still empty, but for the half-empty glass of warm beer. I pushed away another thought, then another, but they were coming faster now. I needed to move; I paid the bill.

Walking made me feel better. I walked fast along Bloor Street, past the apartment where Margaret and I lived with Zooey when she was a baby.

Somewhere on Yorkville, I checked my watch. Only ten minutes had elapsed: It always took me at least half an hour to walk that distance.

What can happen with his mother at the party?

Right, but what happens when the party's over?

I'll jerk him off, she said. No big deal.

I came to a bright, clamoring intersection. I don't know how many blocks I walked. I saw nothing but the furious wallpaper inside my head. I saw Holly sitting upright in bed, facing him, with both hands on his upright cock. Lots of right angles in that room. What would stop her from putting it in her mouth? She'd done it before. I'd seen it before. Why wouldn't she? After all, it was his birthday.

Moving very briskly now, I turned down a side street, cut into the university campus. I needed somewhere familiar, safe. So I headed back to the Other Cafe. I was now going literally in circles.

I came out of a dark alley and turned up Melrose Avenue. The whole street smelt of come. A slow blues guitar wound like a snake out of the second-floor window of a tavern. A black man lamented a cheatin' woman. From where I stood under a maple tree, I could see into the Other Cafe. It was lit up like the Titanic. She was not there. I went in. "Any phone calls?" I asked the proprietress, with muscularly enforced nonchalance.

"You've been stood up," she said. It was just a joke but it left me feeling skinned.

"No, no, no," I broke in hastily, "I'm expecting my daughter."

Sensing something off, an uncharacteristic gravity, the proprietress looked puzzled-friendly.

"Another martini?"

Was she implying I had a drinking problem? Surely she might have said simply, "A martini?" Why "another" martini?

"Why not? Sounds good." I sounded chipper, sporting, fresh from the Land Rover after a day's elephant shooting.

Maybe Holly would tell him about me. The thought made my body relax. I hadn't realized how physically braced I was. She might get a little drunk on champagne and say, "Oh———"—I didn't catch the name again—"I've met this man . . ." A lovely thought, that. But it might hurt him, make her feel sorry for him. "Here, come here. Tell me what I can do for you."

Then an image I'd ducked all night cracked like lightning. A beautiful girl bends over in a blue-lit room and takes a man's cock in her mouth. He brushes her hair away to watch. We both watch.

The martini arrived. It was eleven-thirty.

I eased back down in my seat. "Well," I said out loud, "I'm handling this very well."

I drank the martini. In eighteen and a half hours I could go and find Holly.

And I could sleep for half of that.

A hand touched me on my shoulder. I jumped. It was the proprietress.

"A phone call," she said simply.

I took my time crossing the room to the phone. I wanted to postpone the moment, to bask in it.

It was not Holly. It was Margaret.

"I have exciting news," she said. "Our little noodle is staying the night at a friend's house. A rich friend. Zooey's ecstatic."

Margaret laughed happily, the excitement of a parent who finds herself with an evening unexpectedly free. "I've got money, a car, and no child. I might drop by."

Disappointment pounded like a fist on the roof of a car. I went back to my table. I stared out the window unbelievingly.

What would happen if Holly turned up? Margaret would drive her away in no time. That noxious scrutiny, those infinitesimal pauses, that look of rapt, condemning attention.

I could see it happening.

I couldn't flee. I'd already done that once.

I looked at my watch. By now the party would be over, the guests gone home. Like an old couple, they'd be stacking dishes beside the sink, pouring wine into the sink from squat, half-empty glasses. A cigarette floated among melting ice cubes in an ashtray.

My ex-wife blew into the restaurant. I couldn't speak to her until I'd finished the thought.

Then they'd get into bed; they'd lie in unhappy stillness; he'd turn off the light. I squinted to see what would happen next. In the dark room, her green eyes were open; and sometime soon, her hand would creep across his stomach.

"Say," my ex-wife said, "you're smashed!"

At three-thirty in the morning, I thought this: it takes three years for the human body to completely regenerate its skin; by then she will have outgrown the skin he came on; in three years we'll be free of him. At five-thirty, a rumble of thunder reminded me I was still awake. Rain pelted the roof. It sounded like applause.

Twelve hours later, the rain drifted over the lake, and office girls burst out of the sun at the end of Bloor Street. On the way over I made a deal with God. If she hadn't fucked him, I promised, I'd give up drinking. I drifted through a crowd of tourists. I stopped in front of her table. She looked up; her face was flushed again.

"Holly," I said. Tell me you love me, Holly. "How was the party?"

"Fine," she said.

"There was a crack of thunder last night; it almost blew me out of bed."

"I didn't hear it," she said.

The throng pressed closer. A bearded man stopped at her table, crossed his arms with aggressive casualness. He wanted me to go away. He wanted to talk to the pretty girl with the wide-apart green eyes.

He moved away. I couldn't wait any longer.

"Did you sleep with him?" I whispered.

A vein in my neck thumped.

"I slept in the same bed."

I took a breath. I braced myself again. "Did anything happen?"

She paused. "Nothing happened."

I looked long and hard at her.

"Nothing?"

"No," she laughed. "He's your age. He was tired."

8

*A*nd then it happened.

Holly and I took a taxi to a Jamaican club on the lakeshore. You could feel the air change, freshen, as we drove down through the city; but in the silky darkness I couldn't shake the conviction that something was wrong. The Club Kokua was lit in red haze. Reggae music thumped you in the solar plexus. The place was jammed, black men, white girls locked at the groin. My spirits lifted. We pushed over to the bar; black hands slid a couple of cool gins in front of us. I had to get up early in the morning, the Minister was addressing a convention of small businessmen at two-thirty in the afternoon, he needed some thoughts, but it was too late. I'd already landed in fuck-it land, that boozy place where you think there's something romantic about a hangover, about crawling out of bed and toughing it through the day, dragged out and grey faced. It's bullshit, of course, that's why it only occurs to you when you're loaded.

Holly lit a cigarette. As I reached for my drink, my hand brushed her breast. I felt that same dizziness again. My cock stirred from its lager stupor.

"I like you a lot," she said.

I was tempted to ask it but I didn't.

I pulled her into the mass of bodies; it was hot, I could feel her perspire through her shirt. I tried to dance but it wouldn't come. I couldn't find the beat, I was too drunk, too self-conscious, I avoided her eyes. I gave up, put my arms around her and slid my hand up her back. It was wet. I unzipped my fly, discreetly took out my cock and put it in her hand. No one noticed, no one cared. We moved back and forth, just enough to earn a place on the floor.

I couldn't wait to get home. I took her outside.

I pulled her across the street, down two blocks and into the park that ran alongside the water. You could hear the waves splashing; smell the water. Out in the lake a freighter sat motionless, a single red light flashed bleakly.

"I'm not going to fuck you in a park," she said. I took her behind a tree.

"I'll give you anything you want." I put my hand down her pants.

"God," I said a minute later, "You smell fabulous. Jerk me off. Please."

"No," she said firmly. "Let *me* watch *you* jerk off."

I'd never done that before. But it didn't take me long to make up my mind. For decorum's sake, I tried not to do it too fast. You don't want to look like a monkey out there, thrashing away at yourself with a blurred fist. But you know what they say, there's no touch like your own touch.

She watched intently. "Say," she said, "you've done this before."

On the boardwalk a woman jogger bounced by. She looked over.

We clambered back into a taxi. I was hungry. My heart was pounding. I felt lucid, clearheaded. And also, because of what had just happened, I felt terribly exposed.

That may explain why what happened next slapped me in the face like a shovel. As we pulled away from the lakeshore, Holly fell silent. She leaned against the car door. I reached over and locked it, a gesture she didn't acknowledge.

We drove through the city for ten minutes.

"What is it?" I asked. Right away I knew I'd made a mistake.

"You know," she said, and there was something in her voice that warned me to brace myself, "I'm not very physically attracted to you."

She looked out the window.

"I wish I was but I'm not."

I don't remember getting out of the taxi. I just remember standing on a completely deserted street under a flashing orange sign; it was a dry cleaner's. A streetcar rattled by. I began to walk.

I went to the Circus. All I wanted to do was drink and drink and drink. And I did. I got numb drunk and stared at the mirror. I talked to a hoarse-voiced private detective named Bill. He was a big drinker in spite of an antibuse implant sewn into his liver.

"Isn't that stuff supposed to make you sick?" I asked.

He held up his drink, a short bourbon on the rocks. "I've had six of these and I feel just fine." When the bar closed, we went back to his office for a couple of shots of rye. I fancied I was having an urban adventure. Bill showed me a Smith &

Wesson .38 and some black-and-white photos of dead people; some murdered, some killed in car accidents. Big problems, bigger than mine, to say the least. Finally the rye was gone and so was my interest in Bill.

I took the back streets home. I had a feeling I was going to run into Holly but I didn't. It was a warm night. At the corner of Jennifer Avenue a party was spilling out onto the street. I walked past but a half block later I turned around and came back. I went in.

It was late in the morning when I woke up. The bed was empty, the covers thrown back. I was badly hungover. My face felt like I was wearing a diving mask. I didn't move. I tried to assemble the fragments of the evening. Then I heard something move in my study. I got up, wrapped a towel around my waist and tried to suck in my stomach. A henna-haired girl with bony, freckled shoulders was standing over my desk, stark naked, flipping through the pages of my unpublished novel.

"Oh," she said. "You're a writer."

Now don't get me wrong. I know how that story sounds— like I score every time I walk out of the house. Trust me, that's not the case, or I wouldn't be writing this book. No, I guess that night, God just felt sorry for me and he threw me a fish.

But you know what they say: you got to throw the little ones back.

/9

I didn't see Holly for five weeks. That doesn't sound very long, I know. Even now, writing it, it seems like such a short burst of time. I wonder why I didn't just get on with things, change the tires on my car, put a new plug on Zooey's green banker's lamp. But that's because these days I can barely distinguish weeks from each other; back then I was conscious of the passing of minutes. They had a pounding immediacy, as if, at any moment, she might call, might come up the stairs, might pass beneath my window. And I waited accordingly. So the days were very, very long indeed.

When I say I didn't see her, that's not entirely accurate. I saw her a couple of times but I never talked to her. I was scared of her, of how much she could hurt me, and when I saw her, a kind of panic took hold of me, my body bucked as if I were in danger, real, life-threatening danger, and my thoughts, if you could call them that, locked in a high-speed spin that was out of my control. I walked away from these encounters frazzled, rattled like I'd just been backed against the wall by a snarling Doberman.

Early one evening, it must have been five or six days after I jumped out of the taxi, Spolin and I were walking along Bloor Street. The streetlights had just come on. Ahead of us, in front of an ice cream shop, a young girl stood astride her bicycle, staring, lost in thought, at the pavement beneath her. It was Holly. Her hair had been recently cut, it was spikier than before, and she was wearing glasses; that was new. She didn't look as good, but she looked plenty good enough. I stopped in my tracks and spun about to go in the other direction, but Spolin caught me by the elbow.

"Don't be ridiculous," he hissed and pulled me forward.

"Spolin," I implored, "I don't want to see her."

"Fine, ignore her. But don't run away, for Christ's sake."

Shamed, I followed along. We walked by her, my lips spread like raspberry jam, but she didn't look up. She had the look of someone who was trying to solve a problem in her head, a problem for which she suspected there was no solution. She looked like someone who has lost something but continues to search for it in pockets and drawers where she has already looked.

Of course she may have been trying to remember where she left her red socks or, for that matter, her green shirt. But I was convinced, albeit a tad hysterically, that she was thinking about me. About what to do about me.

I looked over my shoulder. She sat still as a statue.

"The thousand-yard stare," Spolin said. "Not a happy girl."

"I must remember to ask her what she was thinking about," I said.

Spolin snorted with indifference. "You can do better than that, you know."

I was thinking about Holly with her shirt open. "No, Spolin, I don't think I could."

But the sightings were rare; mostly it was waiting, involuntary waiting. There was nothing else to do. One day it would lift, I knew that, but I was powerless to get there any sooner.

So I pined for her. Pined and felt sorry for myself; like an explorer, every morning I put on my raccoon cap and set out to discover new ranges, new tributaries, new continents of self-pity.

I conducted conversations with her in my head until a friend of mine, a woman, told me: "I saw you on the street the other day. You were talking to yourself. Really going at it!"

I made a note to stop moving my lips.

Once, on the street, a man in a fedora whipped around and glared at me. He looked like he was ready to fight. At first I couldn't understand what possessed him. I thought he knew me, somebody I'd cussed out in an after-hours bar years before and forgotten about. But then I realized he must have heard me. So I started to hum. I hoped he'd think I'd been singing. But it didn't work and I burst out laughing. That spooked him worse. I darted down a small lane and had a little laugh all to myself. In peace, so to speak.

At this rate it wouldn't be long before I was quarreling with the morning traffic.

But I didn't phone her. I was terrified of what she might tell me, terrified at the idea of being brought to my knees by a nineteen-year-old girl. "Oh look!" she might say to her young friends. "There he is. Pretend you're not looking!"

I thought about Jonathan; I didn't want to end up like that, a ghost drifting around in her neighborhood, hoping to run into her.

I wanted to talk to Margaret about it, but I didn't. And not for the reasons you might think. Let me put it this way. A few years ago, Margaret had a crush on a man—it was reciprocal—but, for some reason, after a couple of weeks it fizzled. One evening, perhaps insensitively, I asked what happened. And Margaret, with paint-peeling candor, said, "I don't think he wants to take his clothes off and roll around in bed with me anymore."

Margaret had an appetite for brutal truth, but I didn't. Not yet. I figured that when it came to swallowing a hot rotisserie fork, there was plenty of time. Why hurry?

En plus, when she talked like that, it gave me the willies, made me think that maybe I'd made the biggest mistake of my life splitting up with her.

Anyway.

I got drunk at the Bamboo one Friday night and I was kind of hysterically happy. I thought, Oh, what the hell. It's just like calling a friend. I had the phone in my hand before I stopped. Holly and I weren't friends. Sex just doesn't make pals. Not like that.

But this waiting for her to call, it really wore me down; it was like a full-time job. Sometimes at the end of the day, it felt as if an invisible winch was slowly tightening the skin on my face. I lost weight, my eyes shone, my friends said I looked terrific. I went out to dinner with Anna G., a high school math teacher. She looked at me through brown-tinted glasses (Librium, I assumed) and cooed, "You've never looked better." Suddenly I thought maybe I should be with her. We'd been friends for years, but we only fucked each other when we were drunk. Now why was that? I pondered the question and had another drink. Maybe Anna was the solution. I put my hand under the table and gave her knee a little squeeze. After the bar closed, I was afraid to go home, afraid to be in a dark room with my imagination. So I coaxed her into having a hamburger with me. We went to a fast food joint, garishly lit, full of drunks and boisterous engineering students giving hog calls. I took a couple of bites of hamburger and then burst into tears. My friend was terribly distressed. "Bix," she said softly. "Call her. For heaven's sake. Or stop waiting for her to call you."

My daughter won an award for French composition. She got her face in the newspaper; big beaver teeth and a swank, side-parted haircut her mother forked out eighty dollars for. I was very proud. But the devil slipped into my heart and hinted that my having a smart daughter might somehow make me more attractive. I'd call Holly, I planned, and tell her to read the newspaper. "Just look at the People section," I'd say, and hang up.

Forget it.

Coming out of a fruit store one day in Kensington Market, I saw a pretty girl sitting on a cement tree planter; she smiled right at me. I smiled back. It filled me with a surge of confidence. She must have found me attractive. Things were going to be all right. I was going to call Holly and tell her things were going to be all right.

On and on and on it went.

"This is stupid," I wrote in my diary. "You're losing your sense of humor." It was true: As each day wore on, everything wounded me, stripped off another piece of skin. A casual remark, music in the elevator, a corny television show: Everywhere I looked, I saw people in terrible pain.

Of course, I fished out my old diaries, the ones I'd kept when I was Holly's age. I wanted to see what I was like. One entry went like this: "If I don't write something as good as *The Great Gatsby*"—scratched out, replaced by *This Side of Paradise*—"by the time I'm thirty, I'm going to kill myself." I couldn't read any more. It was like eating too much cotton candy.

I was not, I concluded gloomily one evening, a nice or a talented man. And I deserved what I got. Which was, for now, not getting the woman I wanted.

Poor lambie!

In those fine warm summer evenings, it occurred to me that it was only the women who spurned me who really got it right, really understood what I was like.

Dear, dear.

At night, I woke up at three o'clock in the morning and thought about things you're not supposed to think about at three o'clock in the morning: the stuff of an undergraduate's hashish nightmare. I saw myself at fifty, dreaming of Holly, my pants around my ankles, a blistered skin book spread in front of me. "I'll be right up, sweetie!"

Ecce fucking homo.

When I was a tough guy, I dismissed Holly as a self-destructive, mentally ill young person blinded by . . . I don't know, something, mental illness, maybe. My analysis was complicated, sophisticated. But then one night I gave it a tap with a small hammer and it shattered like a diamond. It revealed itself in its stunning simplicity: Holly Briggs was mentally ill because she didn't want me.

Indeed, I was too much for her, too exciting, too vibrant, too threatening a personality.

I heard explosions of derisive laughter.

My ex-wife was right: it did all boil down to who wants to roll around with you.

Two weeks passed.

In moments of opalescent self-analysis, I compared Holly to an antique coffee table with a bad stain. Exquisite, yet somehow ruined. I said to my friends, usually over drinks, "I'm not into crazy girls anymore."

Perhaps in mid-sentence I'd find myself thinking about something other than Holly. But that didn't last long. I missed her body, her taste so much: it was like a toothache, a steady monologue that throbbed day and night.

Of course I thought about creeping up Melrose Avenue and down the driveway. But I didn't dare. The stakes had changed. That wouldn't be titillating, it would be like nibbling on the barrel of a shotgun.

When I passed the foot of Holly's street it was as if there were an electrical barricade that I dared not cross.

But sometimes I couldn't stop myself thinking that right now, this second, maybe she was making love to someone, maybe someone was inside her. Honestly I don't think anything, not even the death of my parents, ever hurt so much. It was simply unbearable.

But I knew if I got over it, I'd get over Holly. And late at night that didn't seem like a bad alternative.

But then came morning: There's nothing like jealousy to make you wake up too early, when there's no one else up, no one to talk to. No one ever talks about just how lonely it is early in the morning. They talk about the nights, but never the mornings.

I looked out the window at the bright new sunlight. I sipped my coffee. A dog wandered down the street, sniffed the pedal of a bicycle and trotted on. He was headed north; in ten minutes, maybe fifteen, he'd be trotting up Holly's street, past her dew-drenched front lawn; I could see Holly roll over in a dark room; she was alone; the curtains were pulled; in the deep-blue shadows Holly Briggs threw an arm back and dozed a moment longer.

Then the waiting started again. I took the phone into the bathroom when I took a bath. I stopped showering; there was a whine in the nozzle that sounded like a phone ringing faintly in another room.

I looked for Holly on the street, in doorways, in the back of a retreating taxi. One evening I was returning from a friend's house after dark. I cut through a small park and found myself at the top of Holly's street. I'd never approached her house from that direction before. I was tempted to turn around, go down another street but my vanity rebelled. I would not be driven out of my own city. I moved down the dark, salt-scented street feeling like a criminal, as if I would be in bad trouble if I got caught. The closer I got to the house, the sexier, the scarier it got. I sped up my pace, I suppose, so that anyone watching might think I was in a hurry to get somewhere, so that if Holly were looking, she'd know I had a destination, that I wasn't coming to see her, that I wasn't sneaking around like Jonathan. I crossed over a tiny street; now I was on her block. A small, silver car slowly passed me and pulled to a halt under a streetlight in front of Holly's house. A figure, a young girl, materialized out of the darkness, she must have been sitting on a stoop, and jumped into the car. I thought it was her. I walked by her house, I threw a glance down the driveway. A faint stain of light, it seemed to me, stirred at the foot.

I went to a phone booth at the corner. Somebody waved to me from the other side of Bloor Street. I dialed Holly's number. It rang and rang. I let the phone fall to the end of its metal cord. Then I tore a sheet of paper from the back of my bank book, wrote "Out of Order" on it and stuck it under the dial. At the end of the cord I heard a faint purring. Still no one had answered. I hurried up Holly's dark street, over the quiet lawns. I turned in her driveway. I stopped and listened. I heard a faint ringing. I went to the window. I couldn't see into the room; the moon was too bright. I saw my reflection instead.

I went around the back of the house and retrieved the key from under the conch shell. I put it in the lock and turned until the door opened, just a fraction. The ring broke clear. I walked into the dark apartment and picked up the receiver. Hello, I said. There was no one there.

I put down the phone. I sat on the edge of her bed. The room smelt of her and it gave me that same dreadful, light-headed queasiness. God, was I never going to be free of her? I pulled back the bedcovers. The smell of her body rose up into the room until I could hardly stand it. I put my face against the pillow. It smelt of her hair. I put my face on the sheets, halfway down the bed. I could almost touch her, feel her. At that very second the phone rang. It startled me like a gunshot. Frozen, I turned to the phone. I knew I mustn't answer. But curiosity overtook me and I crossed the room. The phone jangled; then jangled again. I counted between rings. At last, silence, relief. It stopped. But then it rang again and I reached over very carefully and lifted the receiver from its cradle. I said nothing. I put it to my ear. I listened. There was silence, dead silence that seemed to swell like a bubble. Then it popped and the line went dead and the dial tone hummed in. I was sure it was Holly. I was sure she knew.

Days later, badly hungover, I ran into a friend of mine, a hammer-nosed television producer. His hair was wet, he was wildly animated. He'd just come from the gym; he felt terrific, he said. "I've got so much energy," he practically screamed at me, "my bicycle feels this small." He held up his thumb and forefinger. He was yakking like a lunatic. He couldn't stop. Finally he coughed up why. His wife had dumped him. "Moved out, new boyfriend, the works," he bellowed. He was on top of it though, he assured me. I felt something thud in my stomach. "The trick though," he said, "is to watch the booze. You don't know whether you're suffering from a broken heart or a bad hangover."

I knew what I was suffering from but I also knew he was right. Besides, hangovers are oddly sexy; you just want to eat and get your cock sucked. Brings out the kid in you. I don't know why. I have several theories but they're only fun to describe when I'm drunk.

But I took his advice. I dropped into the Circus a few times, but when you're not drinking, you can't find the rhythm of the people who are. You can't move ahead with them. And I didn't go the other route; I'm not interested in reformed drunks, they're a bore. Whatever it was that took flight when they drank has died.

Another week passed.

I tried going to the movies, sometimes two a night, but my ass hurt, the popcorn made my mouth taste like death, but that wasn't the worst. Sex, the sight of it, made me despair, made me wonder if someone was doing that with Holly. While I had my hand in a popcorn box, maybe somebody else had his hand . . . so I stopped going to the movies.

I started to write a novel. It was about a guy waiting for a girl to phone. But I kept at it, even though it seemed extraordinarily trivial. It kept me company. And, at the risk of seeming immodest, sometimes in the morning I read what I'd written the night before and I liked it. I know you're not supposed to, you're supposed to look at it like drunken sex. But I didn't. I read it over in the morning, in my green chair overlooking the street, and I liked it. It made me feel like I was getting something out of Holly, other than a very, very bad time.

I stayed in town; I didn't go to Europe or Jamaica, things I usually do with a broken heart. I've traveled a great deal; for years I pretended I liked it. But I don't really. It finally occurred to me that I have very little interest in foreign countries and foreign cultures: after all, they bore the fuck out of the people who live there, why shouldn't they bore me? I'm not a bunny rabbit. Things aren't interesting just because I haven't seen them before.

So I stayed in town and wrote my pussy novel. I say pussy novel because that was another plus. It might not make for great literature, although I'm not sure of that at all, but in the course of my "writing," I got to do to Holly all the things I wanted to. The pages curled from the pressure of my pen. And sometimes I worked myself into such a sexual lather that I ended up yanking it out right there, in front of the naked page. I wondered how many other writers have gone the same route; I bet I'm not the only one to jerk off at the work table. You can't tell me Proust did nothing in that cork-lined room for sixteen years except take handfuls of downers and doodle in a scribbler. I'd like to have a look at his outtakes, the pages he wrote pen in one hand, dick in the other. I bet that'd make some reading. But they probably went down the toilet; I bet lots of good writing goes that way.

Then it was down the hall for a peanut butter sandwich. I ate a lot of peanut butter sandwiches while I was writing my novel about a guy waiting for a girl to call.

At five o'clock one morning there was a small fire in the house across the street. The sirens, the whirling yellow lights poured into my bedroom. I got up and stared out the window. I had a terrible feeling that a man was doing something to Holly's body at that very second; an early morning crowd gathered around the fire engine. Then a man, short, high cheekboned, drifted across the street and joined the crowd. He was a real parasite, this guy: he turned up everywhere, I saw him at after-hours bars, P.L.O. rallies, big parties, film openings; he was one of those night creatures who seem to do nothing except go to things. You never see them at work; you never see them with women. I'd never talked to him, I didn't know his name. I'd always ducked him. He felt like a bad omen and you don't have to be a genius to know why. I was terrified to end up like that, standing with my hands in my pockets at five o'clock in the morning, watching the fire trucks pull away. And in that weepy, early morning light, while Holly's green shirt lay at the foot of her bed, it felt like she could save me from it, if only she'd love me.

Then I had a dream (bear with me, it's a short one). It took place at my family farm, long since sold but a place I often go in dreams when I'm unhappy. A thin German girl with buck teeth was custodian; the house was dark, like a movie theater when they turn down the lights. It took a while for my eyes to get used to it. I walked along the narrow upstairs corridor that connected my childhood bedroom with the bathroom. In the darkness, the floor creaked and ached as it always had, and I noticed, or rather sensed, vague movement on the walls. It took a while for my eyes to get used to the dark but when they did I discovered the origin of the movement. Hundreds of small snakes' heads protruded from the walls. Little tails flailed out of sight. You had to turn sideways in the corridors so as not to brush against their tiny fangs.

I protested vigorously to the custodian: it was, after all, my family house.

"They're just decorations," she said with a trace of impatience.

I read Hollywood biographies: Errol Flynn, Elizabeth Taylor, Marlon Brando. I started *Peter the Great* but it didn't give me the comfort I needed so I swapped it for *Merv Griffin: My Story*. Then another night of craving for Holly.

I went to a lesbian poets' symposium.

I saw the man from the fire. He was by himself, too.

When I got home, the green light blinked on my answering service. I played it back. There was a long silence, then Spolin's voice: wired, barely controlled. He obviously hadn't eaten lunch. That's why he sounded that way. I was down the hall, brushing my teeth when it hit me. Maybe that wasn't it, maybe he had something to tell me. The snakes were springing from the can now. I called him back. There was no one home. I left a message on his service: controlled, even. I didn't want to tip my hand.

"Call me when you've got a chance," I concluded in a strangled voice. I sat down in my green chair and stared resolutely ahead. This was a friendship-ender. I thought back to the evening when they'd met, the night we saw *Dirty Harry* together. Yes, even back then I'd had the feeling they belonged together. I must have intuited something. They could have exchanged a phone number while I was in the store; probably not though; they were probably too decent for that, the two of them. They probably just held each other's glance for the instant it takes to express desire and regret and left it at that, knowing, of course, they'd run into each other. It was inevitable, like two neutrons on either side of the universe, sucked slowly together.

Come to think of it, only the other night I'd had a dream about Spolin; he and I had gone to a party at the apartment of two girls and he'd gotten them both. This guy was trouble.

I hadn't heard from him for a long time. A week, maybe two. That was a long time for Spolin. He liked to keep tabs on his friends, make sure they weren't making any new friends behind his back. In fact, the last time I'd talked to him he'd said something odd. He was complaining about being thirty-one, and still having his mother pay his rent. At least that's what he said he was complaining about. He was going to do something about it, he said. He was going to "take charge of his life." Now isn't that the kind of language a man would use if he was on the verge of betraying his best friend?

I began to plan my life without Spolin in it.

Things would lead easily, amusingly into bed; she probably sucked his cock. No, they were meant for each other. They'd exchange secrets about me: what else would two people falling in love have to talk about except my foibles? I went cold with embarrassment; she'd tell him everything, starting, no doubt, with that peeping-tom episode. I hadn't told Spolin about that one. Like a bright soundless bomb, it went off in my head. That's why he was phoning me; he assumed it was only a matter of time before I caught him, before I came lurking down the driveway and hiked myself up on the window for a look-see. And what a look-see that'd be. I phoned him again. The line rang once, twice. I knew there was some profound reason not to go up Holly's street; it must be my sixth sense warning me, protecting me. I inherited it from my mother; she always said, "Listen to your intuition, dear. It'll never fail you." Wise words, wise words indeed!

But he wasn't home. Now that was odd. Why would he phone me and go out?

I was thirsty. I ran a glass of water from the tap; it tasted foul, warm. I had to get through to Spolin. Why wasn't he in? Why is nobody ever in? I rang again.

Spolin answered in a big bright voice.

"I was just about to phone you," he said. "What about lunch? I haven't eaten. I'm starving."

I waited. I tried to interpret, to decode what I was hearing. Was I being set up? God they were setting me up; they were going to give it to me in person. Like a couple of lesbians coming out of the closet, they were going to take me out to lunch and then, taking hold of each other's hands, they were going to say: "Bix, there's something we have to tell you. We've fallen in love." They'd give me a smile like Christians going to the lions. In the background, quite insanely, I heard Holly humming tunelessly, "What's love got to do with it?"

But there was something wrong. Spolin sounded too cheerful; he sounded, I searched for the word . . . hungry.

"Have you seen Holly?" I said.

"Yes," he said buoyantly. "As a matter of fact I have. I ran into her in Just Desserts. She was looking for a job."

It was all coming undone now. I could feel myself winding down like a child's toy.

"So you're not fucking her?"

That stopped even Spolin.

"Do you think I'm insane?"

"Who was she with?"

"Nobody. She was talking to the manager."

"So she just got up and left?"

"Yep. She just got up and left."

"Alone?"

"Alone."

I paused for a moment. I felt a thrill of reprieve. I even ventured a joke.

"She must have been on her way to meet someone."

On my way to meet Spolin for lunch, I wondered, though, if she had been on her way to meet someone. It worried me.

The bad dreams persisted: they always woke me at the same time, five o'clock on the button. "Bix," my long-dead mother called to me one summer morning. "Come in here."

We were in the living room at the farm. "There's a letter for you on the mantelpiece. I'm afraid they've rejected your novel. Again."

Take two: "Bix, come in here please, there's someone I'd like you to meet." On the chesterfield an arrogant young man with round, tortoise-shell glasses. Mother excused herself.

"So," I said settling cautiously beside this self-assured creature, "Have you fucked her?"

"Sure," he said and smiled pleasantly. "About twelve times the first day. Not really my cup of tea."

"And when did this happen?"

"Gosh, let me see." He scratched his head cooperatively. He was handsome. All Holly's nightmare men were young and handsome.

98

"Exactly a week ago," he said crossing his legs. I could hear the swish of expensive material. He gave a loafer a satisfied inspection. "Whew," he said, "I'm pooped," and he gave me a wink.

When I woke up it was with a dread so strong it was as if I'd swallowed a washcloth. I got straight up out of bed and turned on the light in my study and bent over a calendar. I wanted to know what day "exactly a week ago" fell on. I marked it in my diary. I wanted credit at least for clairvoyance.

"A month without Holly," I wrote.

10

Nicholas Beach was a prick. He was also a career civil servant, the Deputy Minister of Industry and Trade. (MIT, they called themselves, hoping to be confused with the real thing.) A grey-haired, fox-faced man, he had a reputation for elegant suits and graceful manners. His staff thought he was classy, "a real renaissance man," one of his aides told me. In the government, if you know who Arthur Rimbaud is, you're classy. But that wasn't why I didn't like Nick. He was a cold fuck, a professional in the worst sense of the word. Behind those classical allusions and "Old World" manners, there was a feeling, an unspoken threat that if you crossed him, even in a minor way, you were finished. There wouldn't be an argument, you wouldn't even know what hit you. Your phone would just stop ringing, and someone else's would start. Nick didn't want brilliance in his writers, he wanted obedience. To tell you the truth, it made me a little uneasy to be in his stable. I wondered what I was doing wrong, whether maybe I wasn't as talented as I fancied. There is such a thing as making the wrong team, but I got a good hunk of my free-lance work from him so I took the poop.

On Monday morning, very early, my phone rang; I waited for the third ring, then I answered calmly, with self-possession, as if I might have been at my desk, writing something decent. I hoped it was Holly. But it wasn't, so I knocked off the silly voice. It was Nick. He had just read my speech to the wood pallet industry, a speech that predicted, for reasons too dull to go into, a hard black rain coming their way. Get competitive, it said, or good-bye; the Americans are going to gobble you up.

"The Americans are going to gobble them up anyway," Nick had confided to me, "but at least this way we can claim we warned them."

He liked the speech but there were problems. Would I drop around at my convenience? That meant immediately. I got dressed, printed up a copy of the speech and read it while I had a coffee.

It was good. I didn't see any problems. But I didn't want any problems either, so I decided to feign an open mind and listen to Nick.

It was on the way over there that I got it up the arse.

I got in my car and drove up a wide, busy avenue. It was a brilliant blue morning and to tell you the truth I was sort of grateful to have something other than Holly to think about. The traffic thickened up and I turned right into the student quarter and drove steadily along until I came to a quick stop. Construction was under way. I turned up a narrow shaded side street. That's when I saw her. She was sitting at a sidewalk cafe with two men; one was the black-haired man, the other stocky, unshaven, wearing a beret. Holly wasn't sitting, really; she lay with her head on her arms, like a bored child, while the two men talked. They seemed oblivious to her.

I pulled by.

At first I felt nothing at all. It simply didn't register. I had thought about her so much that there was something utterly unreal about her actually being there. I drove on another half block, stunned. I absorbed everything—a woman with a cranberry birthmark on her face, a shop sign missing a letter. Then, almost as a luxury, I looked over my shoulder at the retreating table and the trio at it.

When I pulled into the MIT parking lot, I was running, sprinting to keep ahead of my disappointment. I felt like if I stopped it was going to smash me into the ground. I had a high-speed banter with the attendant. I'd never been so friendly. I was like a man converted to Christianity. I asked questions; I listened with bug-eyed attention. I laughed merrily at his well-intentioned but, in retrospect, rather simple-minded replies. I hopped up the stone stairs of the Parliament buildings, two at a time, my heart beating like mad, like one of those chickens that flies over the barn after its head is chopped off.

Then a ghastly voyage down a green hall, a kind of terrible cheap shininess to everything: the ornery blind man selling newspapers from his booth, a woman in a blue dress with too much makeup, a secretary stubbing a cigarette in the sandy ashtray in front of the elevators. I hustled along the hall; I got into the elevator; it was full. We stopped at the second floor. A fat man got in, the fat man I'd seen at the Other Cafe, shoveling the linguini in his mouth. He pushed number three. I wanted to kill him for taking the elevator a single floor. I realized I was holding my breath. My mouth was dry; it tasted terrible. I was afraid to breathe on anyone. We stopped at the third floor; the fat man got out; he took forever getting out. He rested his hand against the elevator door; it started to shut. It bounced off his hand; he made plans to meet someone for lunch. I wanted to scream with frustration. I wanted to plant my foot on his fat ass and kick him sprawling into the hallway. I got out on the fourth floor and sped along the hall. I imagined that once I entered Nick's presence, once the stakes were raised, I'd think about something else. I could escape, never mind for how long, the rat tearing at the inside of my skull.

His door was open; I went in. He extended a cool, powdered hand. I shook it. It was awesome in its impersonality. He wore a sleek grey Italian suit and a cherry tie. Gold cuff links glittered at the end of starched sleeves. His handkerchief, I noticed with some hostile relief, was squared, not ruffled in his breast pocket, a sure sign, my mother once pointed out, of a déclassé.

We sat. There was a problem with the structure, the logic of the speech, he said. And maybe we could tidy up the grammar a little. That annoyed me. He began to outline a new structure; he made crisp, short pencil notations, very faint, on a small sheet of paper. I heard nothing. I couldn't get my mind off the picture I'd just seen of Holly slumped at the table. It filled me with the most awful agony; and it kept getting worse.

He gave me a sharp, critical look.

"Perhaps you should write some of this down."

"Excuse me, Nick, may I use your washroom?"

He paused, just the millisecond necessary to show his disapproval.

"Sure," he said. He put down his pencil carefully and waited. I went into the hall; a robot mailman whirred across my path. I went into the toilet and locked myself in a stall. I used to whack off in these things in happier times. I put my head between my legs and breathed deeply. Then I rubbed my face with my hands. I couldn't stop my thoughts from racing. I looked at my watch. It was only nine-fifteen in the morning: bad news. If Holly was with him that early in the morning, she must have spent the night with him. And if she spent the night with him . . . I couldn't do it. I couldn't finish the thought. I was terrified of the image. It seemed so cruel, so obscene it was almost unimaginable. I took a deep breath. But look at the way they were together. They must be doing it all the time, so much, in fact, that he, the black-haired man, had no particular interest in her, that he was quite happy, quite confident to chat while Holly languished beside him. Worse; she wanted to be there. She preferred to be at a table with a man who had no interest in her than with me.

I pushed it in a bit farther: While I was thrashing around in my sheets with the window open, in case she should come by, with the phone beside my face, in case she should call, she was on her back with her legs wrapped around him.

It was simply nightmare mind-boggling, the enormity of it, a kind of wrecking ball right in the nuts. Now this was overkill.

What a cunt. What a fucking hurtful, self-loathing, sheet-chewing, small-town, blocked, retarded fuck weed.

That was it.

What a fuck weed!

I was craving a cigarette. I hadn't had one for twelve years. Great, she's got me smoking again. I nipped into the hall. A paunchy, tired-looking man in an unpressed suit slumped slowly by. I asked him for a cigarette. Almost grateful for an excuse to stop moving, he stopped, fiddled uncertainly with a side pocket, looking away down the hall, produced a pack, handed them to me, too tired, I think, to extract one himself, and then, after giving me a light, shuffled wearily down the hall and into the office marked VITAL STATISTICS.

I went back into the stall; locked the door; sat down on the toilet. The cigarette tasted fabulous. It fit perfectly into my hand, just as it had twelve years ago. It was like I'd never stopped. I couldn't have Holly but at least I could have a cigarette. The smoke went right to my head. I felt woozy. I also felt like I needed instantly an entire pack of cigarettes. A few minutes later I staggered back into Nicholas Beach's bureau.

He resumed his patient monologue. I was having a hell of a time following him. Finally he finished, put his pencil neatly down beside the paper.

I had meant to be diplomatic, but it had been a riotous morning and I was befuddled by cigarette smoke.

"You know Nick," I said, "there's a reason why the paragraphs in this speech come in the order they do. I don't drop them into a hat and pick them at random."

Nick didn't interrupt. He just listened, an ominous sign.

"And in terms of tidying up my grammar, if you can find one grammatical error in this entire speech, I'll do the whole thing again for free."

The truth is, of course, that I couldn't face dismantling the speech and rewriting it. The monotony of it made me want to weep.

"O.K.," Nick said coldly. He tapped the rubber end of his pencil on the desk and nodded the way people do when they're thinking about something else.

I shook hands cheerfully; but it didn't undo the damage. I

was fucked, I knew it. I'd never hear from him again, but right then I didn't care. I was too rattled. I just wanted to get away, get moving, go for a walk, do something.

Nick looked down at his little square of paper with its immaculate handwriting and folded it delicately in two.

I left the car in the parking lot. I needed a drink. I walked up to the Circus. It was just after eleven when I got there. Ron, the bartender, was just pulling the chairs off the tables. A woman, short, Slavic-stocky in a white smock, was setting up the salad bar in the shadowy corner of the room. She hummed to herself under a cinnamon light. There were just the three of us, and I knew that for the next little while things were going to be all right. I didn't have any illusions about why I was there. I was going to numb the rat. I was going to take the image of a girl with her head on her arms and drink until it floated out of my head, like a big, sunshine-filled beach ball. Ron was glad for the company. He didn't usually see me at this hour.

"Can I set one up for you?" he asked.

"Please. I've had quite a morning."

I took all my money out of my pockets and laid it on the table.

"I'm going to drink until all this is gone," I said, "and then I'm going to go to the bank and get some more."

He slid a tall, gold glass of beer across the wooden bar.

"Cheers," he said.

I bought a pack of cigarettes.

Odd as it may seem, that afternoon in the Circus was a happy time. It had a sort of crazed forward motion, a sense of adventure, of drama to it. There were times when I went to the bathroom and looked at myself in the mirror and felt a shiver of excitement. It was synthetic, but I didn't want it to end and, for a while anyway, I could make sure it didn't. I knew what was in store for me. I've been drunk before, I know the bill you pay at the bar is only the little one, but I wasn't going to tear myself away until I hit the very end of the tunnel. If the hangover was too bad, I'd hit the doctor for a scrip, get some bombers, do a handful and spend a day in bed, watching television.

Then I could muse morbidly, in peace, over my disappointment. All the pathetic scenarios I'd cooked up, all the hundreds and hundreds of conversations leading to all the different ways she might come back to me. And now I realized that I hadn't been on her mind at all, that she'd been preoccupied with an unhappiness that had nothing to do with me. For a month I had wandered around as if the two of us were involved in something. It was absurd, I knew it was absurd and now that it was over I was going to get good and drunk and then I'd take my medicine.

In the Circus, the people came and went. I talked to anyone who spoke English: a fair-haired boy who managed a shirt store, a literate, easygoing fellow who taught English grammar at a community college. Hugh Anderson turned up. He was a plump, bearded, blazered writer who'd made a big splash with a first novel in the '60s; he was an upper-class boy with a wife and two children who went to Montreal, got himself fucked up the ass and wrote a book about it. For a while there, he was hot stuff: he made a literary career of it, the dick up his bum. But a lot of dicks have gone up a lot of bums since the '60s. It wasn't such a big deal anymore and Hugh's work had fallen steadily into eclipse, as his assertions of self-importance grew shriller and more desperate.

"When I suck a cock," he said to Ron, "it's always with an eye to God."

Ron, something of a homophobe, said "Uh-huh," three times in a row and then exploded in pointless laughter. Hugh was replaced by a minister's son who drank four four-ounce martinis, smacked his lips and then, bewilderingly, went back out and sold insurance.

"He does that every day," someone said.

Around four, Ron turned down the lights and I had the oddest feeling it was beginning to snow outside. I was getting blasted so I was very careful with the people I talked to. Very generous. I asked a lot of questions. I resisted the temptation to air my intuitions about their lives, their personalities, their potential. All that, I knew, would eventually lead to trouble. When I moved into a pocket of darkness, I kept my mouth shut, I ignored it until it passed.

The waitresses adopted me. I was their mascot for the day. I hoped one of them was going to take me home.

I avoided bursting into tears when the subject turned to love, when a pretty, small-featured woman, a clothes buyer for a chain store, asked me why I was getting so drunk on a Monday afternoon. It was a close call but I didn't want to wake up the next day and remember weeping in front of strangers, poor Ron escorting me sobbing and slobbering to a taxi. No, things were bad enough without that.

At one point I slipped down off my stool and went over to the pay phone to call Holly. But God made me forget the number; it blew right out of my head and while I was staring into space trying to remember it, I saw an image of myself, a sort of split-screen version of a forty-year-old making a drunken phone call from a bar to the young girl who has just rejected him. It pricked my vanity as if someone had snapped me in the ass with a wet towel. I didn't want anything to do with that, it was simply too unattractive, and I lurched back to my stool. At one point, I noticed in the shadows the arrival of a smart couple in their late forties. They slipped in quietly and sat down in the corner. It was a lawyer I knew and his wife. They were sneaking off for a beer together. Or so I fancied. I liked watching them, I liked the way they were together, the cheerful ease with which they enjoyed each other's company. They'd been married for years, had teenage children. He was something of a barfly and a bimbo-banger and I'd always felt rather sorry for her. She took two hours of aerobics classes a day. But seeing them together, I knew I'd got it wrong or at least I'd missed an essential piece: they were pals, they liked each other, and I had a sad, self-pitying moment when I thought I'd never have that easy rapport, the slang that comes like shared skin from living with a woman for decades.

I was getting a little beer-soggy so I bought some benzedrine from an old acquaintance from Upper Canada College. Honestly, you can't overestimate the benefits of a private school education. It opens doors for you all over the place, just like they told you in prayers.

An hour later, Margaret turned up at the bar: it turned out I had called her. I still can't remember when. Zooey was with her. She brought a Nancy Drew mystery and read it at the bar while her mother and I talked. Margaret bought me a hamburger, insisted I eat it.

Then Spolin turned up.

"It's like magic," I said. "You think about somebody and poof, they turn up."

It turned out I'd called him too.

That set me to thinking about Holly but she didn't come. No magic there. I tried again. I closed my eyes; I wandered around in her apartment. I found her on her bed, in shorts, her knees up, reading a book. I couldn't make out the title. I tried to put the thought in her head, to make her come.

"There's nothing to forgive," I explained to Margaret. "You can't blame people for their sexual preferences. It's like the color of their hair or how tall they are." Margaret lowered my arm. I had been gesticulating. I also had the sickening sensation that I'd hurt her, hit a nerve.

My daughter read on, oblivious.

Holly must have had her transmitter turned down. She didn't come.

Spolin and Margaret fell into a conversation about, I think, Southeast Asia. Geopolitics are not my forte, but I slalomed cheerfully in and out of their conversation for a while. But then, with no one paying attention to me, I grew bored. I gazed into the mirror. It must be getting late in the day, I thought. Things had darkened. My face, cupped in my hand, had darkened. Caught in a quick sideways glance, it took on a kind of bestiality, coarse, malevolent. I looked like someone you should beware of and that pleased me. Then, like a crocodile, the rest of me slipped beneath the water line. Cruel thoughts stepped free. I visualized, quite effortlessly, violent scenarios, confrontations where I backed down schoolyard tormentors. Stephen Love appeared, a cruel blond boy who'd once locked me in a headlock during recess. Like a trapped sea gull I had flailed my arms against his back until he'd pitched me down in front of my passive, even curious friends. The grass had stained my flannels, the elbows of my blazer. I replayed the scene, only now, just before he grabbed me, like lightning I lurched toward him, clasped my hands around his white throat, and squeezed mightily. The image gave me physical pleasure; it filled me with such black excitement that I rose from my stool. Perhaps that was it, perhaps I had not been violent enough in my dealings with the world. Unrestrained ferocity, that's what I needed.

I shifted on my bar stool; this was going well. Beside me, Spolin and Margaret hopped from subject to subject. I inched away from them, from their banal cheerfulness. My face had grown longer, like an African wood carving, a mule or a horse. A drink, a tequila, appeared in front of me. With only the slightest fraction of my attention, I seemed to notice a squint (my, her eyes were small) of disapproval from Margaret.

I dumped the tequila down my throat, replaced the glass very quietly and waited for the explosion. It didn't come. Rather, my thoughts jumped clear of the gloom, the irritating chatter on my left, and landed on their feet. I confronted a teacher who'd told me once, offhandedly, that I was certain to fail my year. I hadn't. In fact, I was now the new crown prince of Luxembourg—a secret blood line had been discovered!—stopping through town to visit admiring friends. I smiled into the mirror.

Fifteen, twenty minutes later I was daydreaming about kicking the shit out of Eddie Grogan when he walked by the window outside. I was sure it was him. I had a wild excited impulse to talk to him. I hurried out onto the street.

"Eddie," I called out. The athletic frame turned. A stern shadow fell across his face when he recognized me, but seeing only friendliness coming his way, he dropped it. His face assumed a sort of wry smile, a surprisingly sophisticated emotion, I thought, for a man like him. It signaled, I guess, a kind of begrudging relief. Eddie wasn't a bright man, but like many lout-heads, he was extraordinarily sensitive and not without a sense of fair play and I think the notion of punching out a half-asleep drunk hadn't sat very well with him. And he seemed to welcome the chance to mend fences. I brought him back into the bar. Putting my hands on his shoulders as if he were my ward, I steered him over to Margaret and Spolin and Zooey at the bar and made noisy, ebullient introductions. I suggested we take a table on the floor and then promptly led the way.

We settled at a round table near the back. It sat beneath a low, copper kettle lamp that bathed us in a rich, golden dust, like card players in a Rembrandt. Seeing Eddie Grogan in the flesh had an enormous, unexpected effect on me. He seemed reduced, diminished. He'd lost the mythological stature he had assumed in my imagination. Eddie Grogan had frightened me badly and on more occasions than I care to admit, I'd woken up at four o'clock in the morning with dreams of gunning him down in the street—the aftermath of which had left me twitching in bed with impotent anger. Plainly, I was afraid of him.

But now here he was, not quite so imposingly handsome as I remembered; strong but thickening at the waist. In fact, I caught myself thinking, if I got it in fast enough, a preemptive strike, so to speak, I could probably take him.

On a less commendable note, I also realized—it had a peculiar urgency—that I wanted to tell him that I'd slept with Holly. It added a dimension to the story which my vanity deemed essential. And in imagining my recounting it, the image it would surely evoke, I saw myself, with great satisfaction, as a colorful literary figure, white-suited, unkempt, a drinker, a womanizer, a man for whom a punch in the face over a woman was a romantic credential.

Our waitress was Mandy, a bosomy, baby-faced sex cartoon for divorced men.

The turn of events—and the fresh company that came with them—gave me a zip of adrenaline and I chattered away merrily. I fancied I was having a marvelous, important time. I seemed urbane, quick-witted. It also gave me a kind of lucidity a triple Scotch couldn't dim. Or so I felt, and ordered accordingly. Margaret, who knew the danger signals, watched me. The talk soon turned to children, to private schools. Margaret was contemplating sending Zooey to a girls' school. But she had reservations.

"The diet's a bit . . . restricted," she said.

Eddie nodded. "She can bring her lunch," he said. He meant well but he was plainly out of his depth.

"No, no," Margaret said quickly. "I mean the company of all those girls, all exactly alike."

Realizing his mistake, Eddie passed a hand sheepishly through soft brown hair. It was an attractive, self-deprecating gesture and it afforded me, or so I was convinced, a minor epiphany, a moment of profound insight into the heart of what seemed by now a remarkable man.

"I like this guy," I burst forth, "I really do."

Margaret rolled her eyes but quickly reengaged Eddie's. She was protecting me, I think, distracting Eddie from my remark. But all that was lost on me.

"Anyway, it's probably out of the question," Margaret said. "It costs a fortune."

"I got two girls at Branksome; I don't have any money left at all. They take everything."

"Bravo," I said and beamed around the table.

Yet Eddie's remark stirred something, some ember of sympathy in Margaret's heart.

I had told her about the funeral, in fact about the whole debacle the day after it happened. She hadn't been annoyed at my pursuing a girl into a bedroom at a funeral, she thought that was "romantic"; but my appetite for getting so blasted I didn't know where I was left her speechless with impatience. A scrubbed, Scottish Presbyterian like Margaret simply could not understand the poetry—I can hear her snort—of drinking till the lights go out. She hadn't met Eddie before but she seemed to have recognized the name. Spolin knew the story too. Driven by fierce, unconscious loyalty, I guessed, he seemed to be sifting Eddie's banter for things to dislike, reasons to condemn him.

Sensing something was off, some peculiar heat coming at him, Eddie turned to Spolin.

"And what do you do?" he asked.

"I write," Spolin said, too quickly.

"And he's the real thing, too," I offered. Spolin looked surprised. I had never given him a shred of encouragement before. But they were all wonderful that day, they were all here, all my friends in the world and we were having a ball. Albeit a somewhat hysterical ball.

"And who publishes you?" Eddie asked. It was just Eddie trying to be in the know, to talk shop, but it caught Spolin in the solar plexus.

"I'm a playwright," he said, as if he'd never said the word before.

"My wife knows a playwright," said Eddie helpfully.

Spolin nodded.

"You know, we sort of look the same," Eddie said. "Same hair."

They did, in fact, but Spolin wouldn't play.

"No, we don't, Eddie. Mine is on my head and yours is on yours."

This was Spolin at his worst, defensive and playing for the house. But he felt the mood at the table turn against him; he was sticking his thumb in the eye of a well-meaning stranger, and it wasn't playing well. And Spolin was very conscious of how things played.

He backed off into mild interest. "What have you got in the bag, Eddie?" he asked. He was referring to a brown paper bag Eddie had with him. Eddie pulled out a brightly packaged video game with STALINGRAD blazed across the cover in fiery block letters.

"Is that for your kids?" Zooey asked, glancing desperately at her mother.

"No, it's for me."

Spolin, who possessed a vast and competitive knowledge about World War II, screwed his head to the side for a better look.

"I don't know why," Eddie said, with puzzled embarrassment, "but every time I get to the Stalingrad part, I get sort of depressed."

This was a code, a war-nut code, and Spolin picked up on it.

"That's where Hitler split his forces," he explained. "That's where he lost the war."

"Pity," Margaret offered bitingly, "he was doing so well up till then."

"He got within fifty-five miles of Moscow," Eddie said.

"Twenty-five," corrected Spolin.

I glanced at Margaret. She seemed at that instant very isolated; there was nothing at this table for her, not really, not anything she needed—not a man, not sex, nothing. It was as if she were just waiting through the afternoon, the conversation, the crowd, waiting for something to happen, to come along.

She doesn't have anything to look forward to, I thought.

"Are you sure it was twenty-five?" Eddie frowned. "That

sounds wrong." It was precisely the right tactic to use on Spolin.

"Positive," Spolin said, with the breathless calm of a man publicly called upon to clarify a point on which he is absolutely certain. "It was Field Marshal von Paulus and the Sixth Army."

Mandy arrived with another round. "A gin martini," I whispered to her retreating back.

"Bix, you can hardly speak," Margaret said.

"That's because the beer is making me soggy," I reasoned.

Mandy returned with the martini. I had a quiet erotic fantasy about her. Eddie leaned back in his chair and in tones that one might use to a longtime secretary asked her to get him some cigarettes.

"There's a machine," she replied with a sweet chill. Mandy was an actress, a model, something like that, I'd forgotten, and she loathed her job.

Eddie handed her a five-dollar bill. "Can you take care of it?" he asked. Margaret frowned. "Menthol," he said.

At this point, I launched into a story about an old girlfriend, a German. It was, in retrospect, a tad threadbare, but Eddie interrupted me. The first beer and the prompt arrival of the second had given his modest intelligence a buff of confidence it might have done better without, and he decided to speak frankly.

"I can't stand Germans," he said.

"Me too," Spolin agreed hastily.

"Well," said Margaret with crisp finality and picked up her glass. It was a trademark gesture. It meant she had no interest in dwelling on this point.

"How can you say that?" protested Zooey with inherited indignation. She looked to her mother for support. Margaret was seeking the right joke, an arrow that would amuse both camps, when Mandy returned through the darkness.

"There aren't any menthol," she said.

She offered Eddie his money back.

"Never mind," he said, "thanks anyway."

"There's a variety store down the street," she said.

"I'll go with you," I said.

We stepped out onto the narrow lane in front of the Circus; a green-jacketed man ticketed cars on the other side. We walked toward Yonge Street. A Trinidadian hot dog vendor closed up his stand. Across the street, a pink end-of-day light scanned the face of the library, a sad, heartbreaking light that cast the city into dramatic lines, sharp angles, burning golds. Two girls in pastels, their arms tanned, crossed at the light.

We passed a record store.

"So how did you end up with a baby-sitter like Holly Briggs?" I asked buoyantly.

He waited a long time before answering.

"My wife smelt that one out, I'll tell you," he said.

My behind contracted once, violently.

"What do you mean?"

"I mean I got into bed one night and she smelt it on me."

A black man broke from the crowd and sprinted across the street. A Volkswagen lurched to a halt.

Eddie ducked into the variety store for his cigarettes. It took forever. When he came out:

"When did this happen?"

"Back in the spring."

"How long? Like a lot?"

He threw the cellophane away. I watched it blow down the street.

"Sure a lot," he said and then was checked by a curious instinct for decency. "No, not a lot. A few times, and then she said forget it."

He laughed, not altogether pleasantly.

"I'll tell you one thing, Bix. That girl will suck you dry."

I walked on a few yards, and then my legs just started up under me. I must have been a scary sight, dead drunk, puffy faced, six feet four, thundering down the sidewalk. A real fucking nightmare.

I dashed across Yonge Street and down into the ravine behind the library. In that deep green ravine I abandoned myself to despair, to the thoughts that, for five weeks, I had pushed away, thoughts that huddled like thieves in the corner of every image, every sensation.

I might as well have slept in her doorway, ghosted her neighborhood like the man in the beautiful raincoat.

I sat down on the ground with a crash. Tears streamed down my cheeks. I opened my mouth and ugly, unfamiliar sounds came out. No, I had a good little sob down there in the ravine but after a while, in spite of myself, my thoughts began to wander. I looked up the hill. A pair of heads moved along the top of the ravine. I could smell the earth; I could also smell something else, something acrid, cat pee, I thought. I looked down. My eyes came slowly into focus. I was staring at a patch of earth between my legs. It moved with tiny white insects, first here, then there. I was starting to get itchy. I got to my feet, crept up the bank and came out behind the library. I crossed the street and slunk along Yorkville, under the eaves of expensive shoe shops and leather boutiques for men. I didn't want to run into anyone I knew. Not now. I'd come down too far.

I staggered into the early evening crowd.

I walked toward the sun; it hung, trembling, at the end of Bloor Street.

I crossed over a bridge. I stopped midway. The traffic poured by. Sunlight glinted from windshields and aerials. I could feel the wind on my face. It was so soft, so peaceful up there. I looked over the edge. It fell away into a deep green ravine. That's where my cousin Scott jumped. He was a tense, eager-to-please man who'd lost a pile of the family money and then stumbled on his wife taking it from behind, all in the same week. That was enough for him. He locked up his office, drove his car to a big bridge, locked the doors, and hopped over the side like an energetic child. It always broke my heart, that business about locking the car. Even in the end he wanted to do the right thing.

Standing up there on that bridge, I didn't have any suicidal pensées, not a one, but there was something black, something ugly hovering in the air, and I found myself dredging up more old adversaries and doing terrible things to them. The eerie thing was that I was sort of enjoying myself, leveling those old scores. So it's not surprising that after a while I started to think about Eddie Grogan.

Then like magic I was back in the kitchen of my house. It was after dark, I was sitting at my kitchen table drinking Scotch. There was a movie running in my head, a vengeful movie. I knew it was a movie, that I was all right as long as I didn't act. But soon I slipped into a quiet, red, murderous rage, so precise, so seemingly lucid, I could have sworn I was sober.

That's when I went downstairs and got my father's shotgun. I wrapped it in a small piece of carpeting, dumped a box of shells in my pocket, turned out the kitchen light and stole back outside. I drove up Spadina, the shotgun nestled on the floor of the backseat. I turned onto Holly's street, I drove slowly past her house. I wasn't a psychopath but I wanted to imagine a psychopathic incident, to follow the steps of one right to the final moment.

I drove through the warm city, up into Forest Hill. I drove very slowly, very carefully. I sucked on a mint in case the police stopped me. I knew I was playing with something very dangerous, but I simply couldn't stop myself. I passed Eddie Grogan's darkened mansion. His red Mercedes-Benz was outside. I went around the block and parked. I put the shotgun in my lap, I reached into my pocket, found a shell, clicked it into the magazine. Then another, then another. It was a pump-action shotgun with six rounds, and I filled it up. Then I started the car again and pulled around the corner. I paused opposite the Benz. I looked up and down the street. A half block up a car was parked on the sidewalk, but there was no one in it. I took one final look, then I eased open the passenger door.

I fired the first round through the window of the Benz. It made the biggest fucking bang I've ever heard in my life. Like the end of the world. A flame shot from the end of the shotgun; the car filled with blue light and smoke. I pumped and fired, then pumped and fired again. Black holes ripped through the car door. It was so violent, so unbelievably loud, it sobered me up in a second. I gunned the car down the street; the passenger door flew shut. In the window of the parked car a man's head popped up. I flew around the corner, but I took the turn too wide, I was trying too hard; the car bounced onto the curb, the headlights illuminating a wildly rocking brown stone house, its lights out. I remember having the incongruous thought that they were probably all away for the weekend at a big cottage; the car rolled across a dark lawn and smacked into a telephone pole. The right front headlight popped. Like an enraged cyclops I sped backward across the lawn, back onto the street and turned up a dark lane. I drove two blocks and pulled the car to a stop. I got out. It was very still. I looked at the headlight. It hung from its socket like an eye. I couldn't drive the car back downtown. Not like that. The cops would stop me for sure. I had a smoking gun in the backseat, gunpowder burns on my hand and the inside of the car smelt like a stick of dynamite had just gone off. There was a kid's bike leaning against a wrought-iron fence. I nipped across the street and stole it. I rode a couple of blocks before my knee hit the handlebars. The front wheel buckled. My jaw broke my fall. I felt my teeth break apart. A syrupy warmth came out of my ears. I wanted to sleep.

People crossed the street to avoid me.

11

I woke up just before dawn. The room heaved with terrors. I moved my head too quickly. A clutch of silverware banged inside my skull. I closed my eyes, curled up my legs. I tried to sneak back to sleep, to tiptoe past the braying in my gut. I tried to summon up an image of comfort, kissing Holly's stomach in the blue morning light, but I found instead other unmentionable things. It was unendurable. And still hours till the day started, till people poured from their houses and milled about in the sunlight. I couldn't wait that long. I got out of bed and pounded down the hallway; the walls shimmered. I went into the bathroom; the bright light stabbed my eyes. I looked in the mirror on the medicine cabinet door. My upper lip was fat, the tip of my nose was skinned. Tentatively, I raised my upper lip. My front teeth were cracked. I had to see a dentist, I had to see him today. But he wouldn't be open for hours, not for hours and hours. I yanked open the medicine cabinet; my face flew away like a startled bird. I found the vial of Valium from the funeral. I shook it. Empty. I opened it. Nothing. I must have done them. I leaned heavily on the sink; the silverware crashed again. How could I have done them all? How could I have done every last fucking Valium with no thought to the future? My dad was right: I am irresponsible.

I went into the kitchen; I opened the fridge; maybe there was a last cool beer. But nothing. I found instead a tiny mocking bottle of vodka, the size of my thumb. I cracked it and poured it down the sink. I went down the hall and sat in the dark parlor overlooking the street. But it was too lonely there, too cold. I went back to bed; I pulled the covers over my head and lay there, listening to my heart beat, wondering why it didn't just stop.

I had to get a scrip; I'd never make it through this one without some help. Trogodons would be just the thing. They're a small white tablet, fun to drink with but a bit destabilizing. You have to watch your tongue when you're whacked on Trogs. It makes you tell people things you shouldn't. Usually I liked to wash down a couple with a cold can of beer and head off to a blues club. But this time it was strictly legit. Pretty much, anyway. I'd wait till nine o'clock and then I'd call the doctor and say I was having trouble sleeping. That much was true, at least.

At nine o'clock on the buzzer, I called. I got the receptionist, a tall, cheerful Brit, the kind who teaches gym in a girls' boarding school.

"I'd like to renew my prescription," I said, using my best private school voice.

"You'll have to see the doctor, Bix," she said.

"Fine," I said.

Not fine. Most unfine. I had cracked front teeth and a very fat lip.

"When can you come in?" she asked.

"Why don't I pop in now?" I said.

This was trouble. Doctor Nathan Glickman was a nice guy but he was no fool. He'd run a methadone clinic in the '60s, and he'd seen my type before. He was not an easy hit. You never knew whether he was giving you the pills because he swallowed the story or because he figured if you needed them badly enough to make up a story, you should probably have them. Scary prospect.

I needed cab fare. I went into the spare bedroom where Zooey sleeps and pried open her piggy bank with a screwdriver. Then I nipped into the bathroom. Brushed my back teeth, brushed my tongue with such manic vigor I gagged like a dog with a bone in his throat.

Glickman was a handsome man, younger-looking than his fifty years. He turned in his chair.

"So," he said. "What's up?"

"I'm having a little trouble getting to sleep."

"Uh-huh." He shook his head absently and looked down at my file. "So you want some Trogodons?"

This was easy.

"Uh-huh."

He swiveled slowly around in his chair until he faced me.

"What'd you do to your face?"

"Tripped on the lawnmower. Almost knocked myself out." I shook my head ruefully, careful not to smile.

"Looks painful," he said.

I shook my head again. There was a pause. I didn't look at him.

"Were you loaded?"

"A bit," I said. Try a small lie to cover a big one. He scrutinized me, then looked down.

"You went through your last prescription rather rapidly."

"*Really?*" I said. My voice went up an octave and I tilted my head to see what he was reading, like a guilty schoolboy called to the teacher's desk to explain an inexplicably high score on a math quiz.

"Did you give any away?" he asked offhandedly.

"Good heavens, no."

I regretted it as soon as I said it. It was open to too many interpretations. It could mean: "Hey, of course I didn't give any away. That would be medically unwise." It could also mean, "Do you think a drug addict like me would give his pills away? Are you out of your fucking mind!"

"Everything O.K. at home?"

"Yeah. Sure. Terrific."

"You and Margaret still O.K.?"

"Yep."

"Zooey?"

"Growing like a horse." An unfortunate turn of phrase.

"Still writing speeches?" A wry smile. Jesus.

"Yep."

"You're not selling these, are you?"

"Heavens no!" I said.

He laughed. "I'm kidding," he said.

He scribbled on a pad. I could feel myself getting happy. It made me talkative. "That's the thing I like about those Trogs, they don't leave me with a hangover."

Hangover. Freudian slip. Who said anything about a hangover? Glickman broke off writing.

"Come again?"

"They don't leave me slurry."

"How many are you taking?" he asked with a frown.

"Not enough to make me slurry."

Slurry. What the fuck did that mean?

"Bix, you're not taking these recreationally, are you?"

I closed my very dry mouth in an expression of, I hoped, mute bewilderment.

"You're not getting off on these, are you?"

He was on to me.

"Getting stoned?" he went on. "You're not getting stoned on these things, are you?"

"No," I said. I shot for a breathy mix of shock and bewilderment and I hit it bang on.

He handed me the scrip. "O.K. Have fun."

"I'm too pooped to have fun," I said. I thought "pooped" an excellent choice. Only an authentically exhausted man would use a word that silly. But it wasn't over yet.

"Last summer you were in here a couple of times in one week. You lost your prescription, was that it?"

"The cap came off in my bag; they got crushed," I said.

He nodded.

"I got rid of that bag though."

"O.K." he said.

I got the message.

Outside the office, out of sight of the receptionist's desk, I broke into a run. I could feel my heart banging with the strain. It had stopped raining; puddles steamed under a bright sun. My running shoes got soaked, I didn't care. I ran right to the bank; then I ran to the drugstore. I was almost home free. I love the smell of drugstores. They make me nostalgic. I caught the pharmacist's eye at the back of the store. He was a stoop-shouldered bald man, very patient. He knew, without my telling him, that I was in a hurry. I'm always in a hurry when I've got a scrip. He handed me the bottle and I did a couple right there, dry.

Remember Harry Chillum? He was my white-haired friend who brought his own vodka to bars. Ten years ago, I ran into a broken-hearted Harry in a bar in Zihuatanejo. His girlfriend, a big-boobed chick, dumb as a tabletop, had just dumped him and he was withdrawing from those tits in the worst way. He couldn't think about anything else, couldn't eat, had his first beer before ten in the morning, chain-smoked. He was a mess.

One morning, early, he knocked on the door of my hotel room. I was changing a Band-Aid on my toe. I'd cut it on the way to the beach and it didn't look very good, despite the seawater. "I'm worried about my toe," I said to Harry. "I woke up thinking about it this morning."

Harry looked absently at my foot.

"Boy, I can hardly wait for the day to come along when I wake up thinking about *my* toe," he said and then started in about his girlfriend again.

But I know what he meant. One morning in mid-July—after I got my teeth capped and the swelling went down—I woke up and I caught myself thinking about something other than Holly's body. It only lasted a few minutes but it was a start, like a fresh wind blowing through a stuffy room.

Later that day I was at the far end of the house, looking down Cecil Street. Mr. Foo tinkered in the garden. It was early evening, the light settled like gold dust on the lawns and the park benches and the leaves. Blossoms shimmered on a crab apple tree across the street. In the park, a round-shouldered woman stood by the swings, half asleep, pushing a little boy. Tired, horny parents eyed each other across the playground. A skinny boy, an adolescent in a long, white T-shirt and a baseball hat shuffled home. I imagined him arriving home, to a house full of voices and rich smells. It gave me a pang, a stab of longing, of missing my own parents. And suddenly I could not remember the last time I'd seen my mother, the last instant. I knew we were in her white house in Mexico, at the end of the Street of Dead Lanterns. I was eighteen, we had just concluded a stormy visit. I was standing in the doorway. I remember she kissed me good-bye there, but did she follow me out into the street where the taxi waited? Or did she go back inside? I couldn't remember and my stomach turned in a quick moment of anguish. If I couldn't remember that last instant, it was gone forever.

At that very second the phone rang. I picked it up.

"I've got a terrible hangover," a girl's voice said. "Would you bring me over a milk shake?"

It was Holly.

I stopped at Harvey's on the way over and bought a chocolate milkshake. I half ran the last block. The back door was open. Holly lay in the twilight on her bed. She was propped against the wall. Her arms were crossed. She was wearing my green shirt.

"I think I've got a fever," she said. "I drank so much I think I've made myself sick."

I put down the milk shake. I put my hand on her forehead. She looked at me evenly. Then I touched her cheek. I took off her glasses. I uncrossed her arms. I unbuttoned her shirt. I started at the top button. I thought I was going to die if she stopped me. I opened the shirt. I put my lips to her breasts. She watched me. She didn't move, didn't touch me. I could feel the heat from her skin. I wanted to lick her everywhere.

"Do you want me to roll over?" she said.

I parted the cheeks of her bum. I ran my tongue along the crack. Then I went deeper.

"Tell me when it's you," I said.

"That's me," she said after a moment. "That's me."

12

*I*t's the oddest thing, but I can't remember very clearly what happened next. It seems preposterous now, to have waited so long, so hard, to remember so much—the quarter hours, the interminable afternoons—*before* she came back—and then so little after. Certainly I remember details, but there's no continuum, no string on which I can bead the jewels. And it seems as if there should be. I wasn't, after all, half asleep.

But it's always like that when you get someone, lose them and get them back. You don't remember, not like you did the first time around.

I heard John Lennon once ask an interviewer to remind him which album came first, *Revolver* or *A Hard Day's Night* and I remember thinking: how the fuck could you *not* remember that? Well, it's perhaps a bit more understandable now.

So: I remember the phone call, the milk shake, the walk over, I remember lowering myself down onto her bed to kiss her but after that . . . the line is shattered. I can't remember if we fell asleep, if we talked, what we talked about. I can't remember the next morning, did we eat breakfast together, did we go out for it, did we have lunch, did I meet her again that night or was it the night after.

That whole new time rests in my memory like a series of brightly painted boxes, big ones and little ones, in which a vivid moment plays itself out, stops, then repeats itself. I'll never know what came the second before or after. But it was, I can hazard this much, a time of extraordinary physical pleasure. I remember taking her to a restaurant one soft night on my motorcycle, the pressure of her hands on my legs . . . it gave things a terrible light-headed urgency; I turned the bike around, drove into a graveyard, stopped, got down, and begged her to come have a look at something I'd found in the bushes.

It was like a virus, something that seemed to grow stronger when I was near her skin. Even the smell of her made me feel sometimes as if I were turning into someone else.

In retrospect, it seems quite silly, undignified, as if I were seized with a kind of dementia near her. Jesus, the things I did or thought of doing or asked for or wanted to ask for. We were sitting on the floor in Holly's apartment one night, she was wearing her paint-stained sneakers, and I pulled her feet into my lap. I stuck my finger down the side of her shoe. She withdrew her foot.

"You can't," she said. "I'm not wearing socks and my feet are sweaty."

"No, let me," I said and I coaxed her foot over and took

off her shoe and rubbed her damp feet with my hands. I rubbed her arches, the pads of her feet. Honestly, I loved doing it, it went straight to my crotch. I would have licked her feet if she'd let me. It's not a big thing, but it meant my appetite for her, for everything to do with her, was still growing.

One night we went drinking at the Select; we got quite drunk, overtipped the bartender and as we were making our way home through the back streets of Chinatown, near midnight, Holly crept down a narrow dark side street to have a pee behind a house. A moment later I went into the shadows looking for her.

"Wait a minute, Holly," I said in a loud whisper, "there's something I want to ask you." And without a blush either. I must have been drunk. But Holly wouldn't play.

"This is loony enough," she said, "without me peeing on your hand."

I'm sure she had a point but I'll tell you, I surprised myself. Baby stuff maybe, but strictly Marco Polo for me.

Some nights, Holly would already be in bed and I'd dash into the toilet for a last pee. Standing over the toilet, I couldn't stop myself from thinking about what was just about to happen. I don't know how many times I wandered into the bathroom only to emerge a minute later, after a dead silence, with a pole for a dick leading me like a divining rod to Holly's bed.

"Christ, what do you *do* in there?" she'd ask.

Once I put a tape recorder under the bed. I don't know why I did it. I still have the tape but I've never listened to it. I'm afraid to even start looking for it. There can't be much on it, though. Holly wasn't a talker. She was extraordinarily silent, that was part of her attractiveness. She said nothing, she just looked at you. I did all the talking and I sure don't want to hear any of that. Out of context, that is. Even as I turned on the tape I imagined some prosecutor years down the road during, say, my trial for tax evasion, clicking that on for proof of moral fiber, my daughter in the front row of the courtroom. Yikes. But at the time it just seemed sort of sexy. Like a lot of things I did with Holly.

"I've never met anyone quite like you before," she said one evening as we emerged from the toy shed behind a day-care center, "there's come on my shirt."

Indeed there was. My heart was still pounding like a racehorse and I was seeing stars.

"Were you like this with all your girlfriends?" she asked.

Alas, no, and curiously enough, in the weeks that followed, there was lots of evidence of that. We ran into Ulana, the slim, big-eyed Ukranian girl who dumped me when I was nineteen. I went to France to find a better girlfriend and when I couldn't, I scurried home. But she'd changed. I returned to a haughty chick who wore golf ball earrings and, my first night back, told me over coffee that she'd never come, not even once, the whole nine months we were together. Wow, what a bitch!

When I introduced her to Holly, I could see she was wondering if I was still up to my old tricks.

We ran into a woman I'd fallen in love with in Jamaica. I was mad for her. She was brainy, pretty and forty-five years old with a breathy, exciting voice. For some time, I thought maybe she'd been ducking me, thought I was mad at her for going back to her boyfriend. The notion that she felt sorry for me —or worse, guilty—filled my stomach with a nauseating mist.

I presented Holly Briggs to her like a retriever does a fetched bird. I'm sure it made us both feel better after.

There was Susan G., a pale girl with a long face and long teeth whose Achilles' heel, sexually speaking, was an acutely detailed fantasy involving doctors in green robes and knitting needles. She was with her husband, a sullen, bearded chap who became even more sullen when he heard my name. It's true that we'd played doctor more than once and she must have squealed.

One morning, when Holly had just left for work, I lay in bed, gleaming with coconut oil, wondering idly, as only a man who has been fucked empty can, if it was possible for me to go through the world, for just one day, without inflicting pain on someone's nervous system. I wrote out a list of all the friends I'd lost or pissed off. It was longer than you'd imagine. But then I crossed off the ones who had it coming and there was nobody left. As for my commitment to gentleness, I forgot it two hours later at the grocery store when I reamed out a Portuguese woman for taking more than five items through the express counter.

But the point is, there was a time there, a short one for sure, where it seemed like I could step into the sunshine without getting bruised. One day, we were folding up Holly's display table, it was late afternoon, when Alain Degat, an old French professor of mine, happened by with his companion. Years before I'd told him, making the necessary substitution, that if I didn't write a novel as good as *Madame Bovary* by the time I was thirty, I'd kill myself. Needless to say, I'd been ducking him for over a decade.

"So," he said, his round, mustached face igniting with delight, "I have you at last. Tell me now, Bix. Where is *Madame Bovary?*"

"She moved out," I said to him. I don't know what I meant by that, but I realized with some surprise that I didn't actually mind if Degat thought I was selling jewelry on the sidewalk, and I wondered for a second if I had at last outgrown the excruciating vanity that has made me drop a newspaper like a rattlesnake at the mention of a friend's success.

No, for a while there, I glided through the world with impunity. I was afraid of very little: no rebuff, no cold reception. It was therefore an excellent time to mend fences; there's nothing like the largesse that comes with nothing at stake. To wit, I looked up Jeremy Jenkins. He was a short, pink, happy man given to bursts of squealing laughter. I liked him—he was the best copywriter in the country—and I wanted to work for him, but years before I'd insulted his girlfriend at a party and he hadn't spoken to me since. But late one Friday afternoon I swept into his office full of breezy self-deprecation, and twenty minutes later he gave me a little bank brochure to write, not a big job, not a lot of money, but a small bridge back to the world.

There were other minor triumphs; I lost graciously to Margaret at backgammon. Normally it makes me want to beat her up, but during this little spell with Holly I'd just sort of close my eyes and think about licking Holly under her arms—and I could feel the fury evaporate.

Other victories: I didn't hit up Dr. Glickman for my mid-summer scrip. I didn't like the idea of being stoned, rubber-lipped and sloppy around Holly. So I let it go.

And since I didn't have any pills to counter the hangovers, I stopped drinking too.

I even contemplated paying back my student loan but when

I found out it was three thousand bucks I realized I had gone too far.

One night Margaret went out of town and I had to work late, so Zooey stayed at Holly's. They were almost the same height, and I came home late to find them hot-footing it down the street together. It was after midnight, the street was deserted and they were having a foot race, these two young girls, racing soundlessly along the sidewalk, their beautiful white nightgowns trailing behind them.

And yet, and even now I'm reluctant to say it, there were little things, moments that rankled, that made me feel suddenly very alone, that made it seem as if someone had forgotten to wrap a towel around the clock and we could both hear it ticking. Holly met me at a restaurant down on Queen Street for dinner. She was wearing glasses and I had the nagging, rather gloomy thought that you don't wear glasses to see someone you want to find you attractive.

And to be truthful, even with me things were different. Let me put it this way. When I was a kid, I spent my summers in a big white house overlooking a field that rolled down to the lake. When I think about those times, I remember sleeping past noon, I remember hot yellow sunlight. I also remember a clear view right to the edge of that blue lake. In my mid-twenties, I inherited the house. I moved my stuff—my furniture and that awful novelist girl—into my childhood home. And right off the bat I noticed something different. Except it wasn't different. It had always been there. The field, near the bottom, was a mess of hydro poles. Power lines, black and thick as an arm, crisscrossed the property. At night you could hear them hum with megawatt voltage. My property must have been the converging point for the electrical needs of the whole fucking community. Anyway, from that day on I couldn't look at the field or the lake beyond without these giant black wires falling in front of my face. I'm not saying the same thing happened with Holly. But I observed in myself disturbing seeds. When I was making love to her once, I noticed with a very mild distaste a tiny blemish on her shoulder blade. It was the first time I had discovered something wrong with her, something that, however obliquely, I wished different.

It was nothing, the blemish disappeared the next day, but I knew the fact that I had noticed it meant that things were changing. That I was getting used to having her. Even the most extraordinary circumstances, it seems, only take us out of our lives for a short while.

But there was more to it; there was, in my reaction to this blemish, a sense, however faint, of relief. It was as if I saw in it—or rather, in my reaction to it—a way out, an escape, if need be, from the frying pan. What would it take, how much would it hurt? Sometimes, during a walk by myself or a private moment looking out the window, I imagined looking in Holly's window and seeing another body with her, the sheets moving in the dark room; and I found myself wondering, to the point that my lips moved, what I would say, what I would do. There was a level, a rather cold one, I realized, of self-protection that hadn't been there before.

It came out in ways of which I was only hazily aware. We went for a motorcycle ride. We were in August now; a certain clarity of light hinted at an early fall. I lent Holly a black leather jacket; it was shiny and short-waisted, slightly too small for me. "It must have shrunk," Margaret said with some amusement. "Leather does that."

It had a high collar and Holly looked smashing in it, better than I did, of course. She was better looking.

It was a pink, sunset evening; we stopped at the Select and had a beer at the copper-tinted bar. It was an intimate little corner, dark wood, big leafed plants, scents of garlic and basil wafting from the kitchen, Billie Holiday suffering quietly from expensive invisible speakers.

"It's like the Circus," she said.

"What do you mean?" I said.

"I mean you like dark bars."

"That's because I look better in dark bars." I thought it best to say it first.

An old girlfriend walked in the front door, looked right at me and kept walking. It wasn't until months later that I remembered seeing her.

I ordered a musty German beer I'd never heard of, surprisingly expensive. Holly looked straight ahead at the wine basket, the black jacket accentuating the sharp angles of her face. A dripping jewel, I thought. She evoked in me the same inexhaustible fascination my daughter did: I simply couldn't look at her enough, couldn't neutralize the *fact* of her.

She took a sip of her beer.

"Ah," she said, "scent of skunk."

I can't remember why but we were spending that night apart and a couple of hours later, it was dark now, I puttered up Melrose Avenue, Holly's hands lying lightly on my thighs.

We pulled to a stop. She took off her helmet and handed it to me.

"Do you want the jacket too?" she asked. She asked lazily, like a bad waiter asking if you want change. It had something of the same effect.

"Sure," I said, too cheerfully. "Let me have it back and then, the next time we go out, you can have it again," this delivered as though I were thinking my way aloud through a complex problem. Holly shrugged, I think she shrugged, I couldn't see for I had lowered my eyes. I had the feeling if I let her keep it that night, she'd keep it for good. And the truth is, I didn't want her to have it, not that way, not just casually assimilated into her wardrobe. Perhaps there was more to it. Perhaps I equated giving it to her with losing it. Besides, I reasoned, it'll smell like her now. Some day, when she's gone, I can pull it off its hanger, open it up . . . It was, I realize now, a minor stockpiling for life after Holly.

/13

*T*hen one night we saw him. Or rather I saw him. It was after dinner. Holly, Zooey and I wandered through the Annex. Zooey wore a red dress and new rimless glasses; she held onto Holly's arm with both hands, talking animatedly. She was attracted to Holly, freer with her, physically, more at ease touching her than I was. Holly liked it. She liked Zooey's bursts of uncomplicated affection, her appetite for fun. I browsed happily in their wake. Zooey was absorbed in telling Holly a schoolyard drama, the story of a classmate with huge boobs (her term) named Eddie and Freddie, respectively. When Zooey got to that part of the story, laughter wrinkled her face and bent her stick body in two. It gave me pause. A drawer of new sophistication had just popped open, sometime, I was sure, in the last week or two, and for a second I stared at her as if at a stranger. Zooey ducked into a bookstore. Holly followed her. I waited outside, watching people pass by in the languid summer evening. A car pulled up in front of me. It was a silver-grey Audi, very shiny, new-looking. Inside, wearing a crisply starched dress shirt and a flowered tie was the black-haired man. For the first time I noticed how good-looking he was; his chin was well cut, his teeth white and strong, and a nose that beaked slightly at the bridge. It was a face that belonged on an ancient coin.

He was listening with benevolent confidence to a young girl. She had exaggeratedly white skin, and her hair was cut in a black bowl. She was talking energetically and happily. She was excited to be where she was.

The light changed; the car pulled into summer rumors.

Zooey and Holly emerged from the bookstore. I said nothing about the silver-grey car, but I wondered if I should. Years before, ten at least, I'd been holding out on a cocktail waitress; it had been a phone war, a test to see who would crack first. We had had a tiff, it had happened many times before, we quite loathed each other, but this time it dragged on and on. Weeks passed, then a month, then two months, until a well-meaning friend, a lanky walleyed fellow, bushwacked me over a beer one afternoon. He told me he'd called her house one morning very early, looking for me, and a man had answered. Well, it blew me right off my bar stool. I went into a devastating tailspin, drank too much, called people I shouldn't have, and so on and so on. But the curious thing is that it was only at that point that I began to get over her, the moment I heard she was in bed with someone else. That was when I started to get better.

So I wondered whether the same thing might work for Holly. Risky business, though. It could backfire, could drive her right back to him. But, I reasoned, he's got someone else; now is the time she's likely to be turned away, forced to get over him. Still, when I looked at her walking down the street with Zooey, she seemed like a child and I couldn't stand the idea of hurting her.

But later that night, I slipped into the bathroom and looked at myself carefully in the mirror. Left profile, right profile. It was, as a friend once put it, as if someone had turned up the heat at Madame Tussaud's. Not an encouraging spectacle, especially in the wake of Holly's aristocrat in the shiny car. For a second I felt a keen sympathy for anyone who had ever balked at fucking me. I came out and started down the hall but ducked back into the bathroom and peered again at the mirror, the way you get off the scales and get back on again in case they were wrong the first time.

I sat down heavily in the chair that overlooked Cecil Street. Hand-sized leaves waved up at me. Across the street, a teenager furtively slipped a coat hanger down the window of a parked car. He looked around like he was taking a pee, caught me staring at him, pretended to zip up and disappeared down the street.

I told her a couple of nights later, in a moment when I feared she found me dull. We were in a restaurant, I can't remember even where we were, just that in mid-sentence, I felt her interest in me fizzle, and suddenly I was sitting across the table from a stranger, remote and cold and monosyllabic, and to get her back I said, brightly, "Does your friend have a daughter?"

She looked up; a look of distress passed over her face. I could feel something start up in her that I hadn't counted on, that she couldn't stop.

"Why?" she asked.

The waiter returned to clean the ashtray. He wiped the table. Holly looked around his arms to get back more quickly to the conversation. She reached very deliberately for her beer.

Then I told her.

"What did she look like?"

"Like Scaramouche," I said, pleased to have pulled down so adept an image.

"Don't editorialize, all right? Just tell me," she snapped.

I described the girl in the car. I smiled foolishly. "I just thought he might have a daughter."

She gave me a look of undisguised loathing.

Was it that night or the next?

I was in my study. It had now been four weeks since I brought Holly the milk shake. She was sitting in a chair near me, flipping through magazines. I was putting the final touches on a Barclay's Bank brochure. Working on a little joke, talking to Holly, trying the various tag lines out loud. At one point, almost unnoticed, she put down her magazine and slipped out of the room. I heard her footsteps in the hall. I thought she was going to the bathroom but she passed right by into the kitchen. I heard the light switch click, I heard her settle in the dark in the rocking chair beside the window. Then silence.

A day, two days later. We had been asleep for hours when suddenly Holly began to cough. I put my hand on the nape of her neck. She was perspiring.

"Are you ill?" I whispered.

She put out her hand harshly as if to silence me and another round of violent hacking shook her body.

I went to an all-night drugstore to get her cough syrup. That quieted things down so she could sleep, but at five-thirty, around first light, it started again. She threw herself forward in bed, her eyes filled with tears. Holly never cried.

She rested her head on her knees. I lay down on the floor beside her to give her the bed, and she fell sound asleep. Whatever the poison was, she had expelled it.

Later, when I woke up, she was sitting in my green chair, overlooking Cecil Street.

"Bix," she said. "Do all girls taste the same?"

I didn't understand.

"You know," she said.

"More or less."

I heard her get up. It was the middle of the night, very quiet on Melrose Avenue. Very still. I heard the kitchen door click shut. I heard the phone get picked up, I heard a couple of numbers being dialed, then I heard the phone click back into its cradle and there was a long silence. I tiptoed down the hall. Holly sat naked, staring out the window.

"Who are you calling?" I asked.

The next night, I was asleep in bed. At two-thirty in the morning I heard a car door slam and then the glass in the downstairs door shivered. Footsteps took the stairs lightly, two at a time. They paused at the head of the stairs then started down the hall. The floorboards creaked and groaned.

It was Holly. "Is Zooey here?" she asked.

"No," I whispered and pulled the sheet back for her. I heard her jeans unbutton, the zipper went down, the pants fell to the floor; then a softer sound, cotton on wood as her shirt landed beside them and then the bed sagged with the weight of her young body. She had been drinking. I could smell red wine. Holly's mouth tasted wonderful, like a bouquet, when she drank red wine. I could feel her hands reaching for me under the blanket.

"My hands are cold," she said as she eased me over onto my back.

At first I didn't know what it was. It wafted up from the covers.

"Holly," I said, "what is that smell?"

She stopped, frozen, and popped her head out of the covers. One look at her face and I knew. I pushed her away. She pulled the sheet over her breasts and looked at me.

"I can smell it Holly."

She opened her mouth to speak but I jumped out of bed and crashed down the hall and went into the bathroom and turned on the bathtub tap and then I went back and slammed the door hard. I ran the water hot and then I got in, even though it was still too shallow. When I turned off the tap, I listened, my heart pounding. I heard her come down the hall; she went into the kitchen; she opened the cupboard; she got a glass from the cupboard and filled it with water. A moment later, dressed—it made me despair to see her dressed—she appeared in the bathroom, the glass in her hand.

"You fucked him, didn't you?"

She didn't answer. Just looked at me, scared and guilty.

A black fury seized me. I leaned over and smashed the glass; it flew out of her hand, shattered against the porcelain and fell into the tub. I was just about to reach for her, to grab her by the shirt and shake the living piss out of her when she stopped me dead.

"Don't move," she said. "Stay still." She was looking at something to the right of my leg. Her tone frightened me and I looked down. The water was turning crimson. The two of us sat there in the bright frosted light and watched the bathwater turn red. I lifted my hand out of the water; blood dripped freely from a jagged rip an inch below my baby finger.

"You've got to go to the hospital," she said. Blood streamed down the side of the tub.

"You fucked him, didn't you?"

The blood in the water was making her frantic.

"Tell me," I said. "I'm not getting out of this tub until you do."

"You've got to go to the hospital," she said.

I didn't move.

"Yes," she said finally. "Yes, I did."

I took a long deep breath, my nerves screeching. I looked down at the water.

"It looks like a murder in here," I said.

I put my feet on the hot and cold water taps and boosted myself out of the water. Holly wrapped my hand in a white towel. I started talking about Émile Zola, I don't know why. To impress her, I think, although I imagine she was pretty impressed already. We took a taxi down to the emergency room. Holly was pale as a dirty sheet; this was not her kind of thing at all. A tad too confrontational. I'd never fully realized how passive she was, and in that green hospital light, it diminished her, made her seem insubstantial.

I got sewed up. My finger, my baby finger was numb. The doctor said I'd severed the nerve. I asked him how long it'd be before I got the feeling back, and he said, "About ten years." I looked for the joke.

He nodded. "Nerves grow very slowly," he said.

"Can I have something for the pain?" I asked. Out of habit, my eyes flittered guiltily in mid-sentence, but the doctor gave me a scrip for four days of Percodan.

I did two in the taxi. By the time I got back to Holly's I was starting to get off, and twenty minutes later I was flying. The water had drained from the tub; there was just the ghost of a red smear left. Floating on a Perc wave I lay in her body-smelling bed, my hand bandaged.

"I'm sorry about all this," I said, in a weak theatrical voice. It was, after all, only six stitches, but I lay there like the dying Prince Andrei. She just nodded and raised her eyebrows.

I lay in Holly's bed for a couple of days. I called a couple of people I had work for; told them I was sick and got extensions. It was the first time I'd called in sick and it had a kind of cathartic beauty to it, being that it was on the level and all.

Holly didn't go to work either. It was unspoken. The pills made me sweaty and sexless but very talkative—I felt like a chatty eunuch—but they kept the pain from my ripped hand at bay. Sometimes I'd wake up from a nap and I could feel it pulsing.

On the third day, Holly went to the corner to buy a quart of orange juice and the phone rang. Somebody paused and then hung up. He was getting closer; I didn't have much time. When she came back with the orange juice, I asked her to take a little trip up north with me, just for a couple of days. She weighed it for a second.

"Are you sure you're up for it?" was all she asked.

It was the last weekend of the summer. We took off late Friday afternoon. I left the pills behind. I wanted to be clearheaded for this. My hand started to ache, but that was a good sign. I could feel the blood returning to my groin. We drove up through the city, through Forest Hill Village; I took a little detour and we drove by Eddie Grogan's house. A black BMW sat in the driveway.

"Eddie's got a new car," Holly said casually. She looked

over at me. In the fading sunlight, the sleeves of her shirt ruffled in the wind. She shook her head, it was a very small shake, very slow, very Holly.

We drove on a bit. Then she spoke again.

"I want to go back to school," she said. "I need a letter. Will you write one for me?"

"Sure," I said. "Anything."

"Sometime after we come back." She said it like that on purpose, I think.

We passed through the outskirts of the city, a realm of car dealerships, fast food joints, gas stations, and giant, strutting hydro poles. A mustard-colored cat lay dead by the road. To the right, a field had been skinned by bulldozers and lay exposed like a wound. Holly ran a hand through her hair, holding it off her forehead. She was squinting.

"You should get sunglasses," I said.

"I know."

"Why don't you?"

She thought about it for a moment, scratched herself under the chin.

"I had a nail in my shoe last year," she said. "I walked around for two weeks complaining that my foot hurt. Then somebody finally said, 'Get your fucking shoe fixed, will you? It'll take five minutes.' "

"Did it help, somebody telling you that?"

"No," she said a little coldly. "It didn't help at all."

The city, the factories fell away. Straw-colored fields spread on both sides. Grain silos rose across the fields. She turned on the radio.

"Do you think you'll ever get married, Holly?"

"I don't think about it."

"What do you think about, Holly?"

"I think about why I never do anything."

A white jet ran parallel to us in the pearly blue sky. She leaned back in her seat and straightened her back, lowering her chin like a cadet at attention. She put a foot on the dashboard. She was wearing the paint-stained running shoes.

"You can take your shoes off, if you want."

She smiled. "You must be feeling better."

She took her shoes off and put a bare foot on the dashboard.

"Did you ever paint your fingernails?" I asked.

"Not for a while."

"When?"

"A couple of Christmases ago."

"What was the occasion?"

"Just fooling around." Then, as if she understood, she added, "There was just my brother and my mother and me. Just the three of us."

"What color was it, the nail polish?"

"Clear. Or a light pink. I can't remember."

A hill rose sharply on the right. Pine trees ran along the ridge like straightened teeth. The sunlight fell gold on the countryside.

The landscape changed. The ennui of flat farmland vanished. Trees, rocks, cabins came closer together. The road narrowed, swept into a gulley, past bait shops, prosperous motels cut into the rock. A bright Canadian flag flapped from the roof of Mom's Restaurant. Cattails rose from green marshes, a song came on the radio, a chirpy twenty-year-old song about love being like a red rubber ball. The last sunlight played on Holly's shoulders and bare arms.

Then abruptly, like a door shutting, it went dark. I can't remember what we talked about, I just remember Holly's voice, it was the damnedest voice, like a knife tapping the side of a crystal glass; she just looked straight ahead and talked, comforted, I think, by the darkness, by the occasion that neither of us acknowledged, at least to each other. As a child, I'd found this trip north interminable, but now I wanted it to go on and on, just rushing through the dark with the sound of her voice fading in and out.

"Where are you, Bix?" Holly said. "You're moving your lips."

"What was I saying?"

She shook her head. "You were frowning."

She put her hand on my forehead and I could feel it relax.

She put her hand out the window, flat against the wind and then swooped it up and down.

"A wind fish," she said. "He's been following us since we left town."

I looked over at her. She was happy.

We were almost there; we swung east, running flat against a black lake. Under bright lights, condominiums perched like grey cats on the shoreline.

We pulled down a white gravel road, the headlights bouncing down toward the lake, through a copse of pine trees, up onto a big billboard. Friendly Acres, it said; it showed a picture of a man in a hammock. My family house, long sold, was just down the road. One night, when I was about fourteen, my mother, fed up with a household of men, had run away. She jumped into her grey Dodge, drove a couple of miles down the road, and checked into Friendly Acres. And when my father and I came to fetch her in the Morris a week later, I could see why. It was the perfect place to go: big windowed cabins, empty lawns that rolled down to the water, quiet meals in the main house, a shuffleboard court, an unsinkable green canoe. . . . It was rather like a lush insane asylum in the country and I remember thinking, even then, that it would be a great place to take a girl.

We got there around ten o'clock. They had a cabin ready, called Love Dove 2. It had one bed in it, which smelled of clean sheets and pine and had feather pillows, and you could hear the lake lapping on the dock.

It was a jewel for a morning; we walked across a dew-bright lawn to the main house for breakfast. The birds chirped tentatively, as if unsure of the hour.

We had pancakes, mounds of toast, all that country stuff. There were other couples, mostly older folk, a red-haired man named Vern and his mother—I gathered they came every year—and a couple of solid-looking gals who worked for the hydro company. Outside on the lawn, a small child with curly white hair, a baby really, tottered barefoot across the grass while a pregnant woman in turquoise shorts called after her.

We went back to bed after breakfast. She left her shirt on when she got into bed. It made her eyes very green.

We went for a canoe ride. We paddled right out into the middle of the lake; Holly slipped over the side and handed me her T-shirt. She was always so shy, in such an odd way. It was kind of flattering. Suddenly there was a flurry of little boats, bright-sailed sunfish; we were in the middle of a race, all these beautiful little boats clipping by on the blue water and Holly hanging onto the side of the boat and the boat just drifting out in the center of the lake.

By six o'clock, long shadows stretched across the lawns. A boy in a white shirt blew an English horn, long and silver, to announce that dinner was ready. As we walked across the lawn, Holly put her arm around my shoulder; she had to reach up, way up, it couldn't have been very comfortable but it was the awkwardness that made it so touching. I loved the weight of her arm.

Vern had seen a car accident that day; everyone listened to his account. "It was a two-vehicle crash," he said with expertise. A sea gull walked by on the lawn.

That night we went for a long drive; bats swooped for white moths, a canoe drifted along the shore. We rolled along asphalt roads, Holly staring straight ahead, the headlights illuminating savage green trees, a tune on the radio, country and western, a guy singing through his nose.

I gave my soul to Jesus,
I gave my heart to you,
If you want the rest of me
You can have that too. . . .

Down that country road, Holly's voice in the darkness, the tinkle, a ring of echoing crystal.

Her monologue meandered here and there, it paused on her childhood, a ruined coloring book, a red-haired boy who'd hugged her once, rashly and impetuously; a failing report card. On it went and it seemed odd that now, just as I was about to lose her, I was getting to know her.

"All my memories," she said, "seem to land on the left foot."

After a moment, I said to the silhouette, "Do you know how attractive you are?"

"I'd trade it for a good job," she said.

Down that long dark lane we went, that ringing soft voice

talking and talking . . . She sat slightly turned in her seat, her body toward me, her face straight ahead.

She fell asleep quickly. I just lay there, listening to a voice across the lake. I didn't want to sleep; I didn't want to miss anything. There'd be plenty of time for sleep. After a while I got up and slipped outside into the fresh country air. I started walking. I walked all the way along that dark country road, I walked for two miles under the moon. When a car came, I saw the lights on the trees ahead, and then, after a while, heard the tires on the pavement and I stood well back from the road and then the car lights appeared blindingly bright; they raced along the deserted highway, dipping as if in surprise when they caught me in their glare, and then the car blasted by. I walked past the graveyard. I was getting close. I turned onto the old road and walked a hundred yards and turned down a tree-shaded lane, it was almost black in there, I could hear the stones tumble under my shoes. I used to walk along this road at night, my heart pounding, waiting for a killer to reach out from the dense foliage and pull me in. It was the worst thing about going to a summer dance, that last hundred yards before home. But now, I didn't feel anything; I almost wished something would happen. I came to the top of the lane; the forest broke. I looked down on an immaculate white house. A light was on in the living room. I stood on top of that hill and looked down on that white house in the moonlight. That's where I'd lived with my family. And now, twenty-four years later, in the middle of the night, I had come back. But it was somebody else's house now. I looked beyond the house; I could see all the way to the double-mooned lake. I couldn't see any hydro wires. Not anymore.

I found myself thinking about Georgina Buckley, the potato-nosed girl I adored when I was fourteen. I got over her in that white house. She was my first girlfriend, my first kiss, I think, during a movie. She lived on Orville Crescent and I used to bicycle over there after school every day; it was a ritual, one of those things you take for granted. Anyway, Georgina broke her leg and while she was in the hospital I played spin the bottle with her best friend Rodent, a self-adoring little puppy in a red sweater. So when Georgina heard about it, which she did the next day, she burst into tears, her little foot hanging stiff in the air, and she dropped me. She dropped me for my best friend, Tommy Crane. When the news got back to me, the news that I was dropped, it didn't mean much. I sort of didn't get it. Not at first. But then it hit me. It hit me that I was never ever going to have the chance to ride my bicycle over to Georgina's again. It was like a crumpling body blow. I ducked into my mother's bathroom, just beside the window with the light in it, and I had my first little weep over a girl. I was never going to ride my bike over to her house again. Really, it was too sad. Then my holidays ended, school started again. Tommy walked Georgina to school. I hung around with Rodent. Everyone thought it was cute. But it wasn't, you see, because I liked Georgina and Georgina liked Tommy and Tommy liked Rodent and Rodent liked me. So you see, nobody got what he wanted; it was like everyone got somebody that somebody else wanted. We were only fourteen and it had started already.

When I got back to the cabin, I went down to the dock and wrote Holly a letter of recommendation. It seemed like an odd thing to do, that kind of language for someone you're in love with, but I did it and then slipped it into the bottom of her bag and got into bed.

"You know," she said, just before I fell asleep, "we should get the screens on the window fixed."

"What screens, Holly?"

But she didn't answer. She was talking in her sleep.

I went back to bed after breakfast the next day. I was exhausted. It was like waiting for rain. The lake was still as a tomb. Even in the country you can feel the pall of Sunday; it's like death.

Holly went down to the dock to read. I woke up around eleven o'clock, my face wrinkled from the pillow, and staggered out into the dazzling sunshine. Holly was sitting in a chair at the end of the dock; she had a book with her, but she wasn't reading it; she was staring out across the water at a big green boathouse across the bay. I went up to the main cabin, told them we'd be leaving early in the morning, and settled up.

14

I dropped Holly off at her apartment. I didn't
go in. I went home and slept. When I awoke it was after five
in the afternoon but it felt like winter outside. I half expected
to see huddled figures rushing through the snow. I called
Holly's number but the line was busy; it felt urgent. I had to
talk to her. When I got out on the street I was relieved; there
were people everywhere. I called her again from the corner
phone booth. The line was still busy. She must have taken
the phone off the hook to nap.

I got into my car and started up through Chinatown; red
and orange lights flashed over restaurants. It was rush hour. I
turned up that winding street and sped up. I was going too
fast and I knew it. A little girl in a white T-shirt pushed her
skateboard, one foot on the street, one foot on the sidewalk.
I gave her a honk. It made her little body jump with fright

and I instantly regretted it. "Sorry," I hollered through the window as I roared by, like Ahab roped to the side of Moby Dick.

I parked the car nose first, jumped out, walked briskly across the lawns of two houses and started down Holly's driveway. I was almost there. Her window was open; she was on the phone, her back to me. As soon as I heard her voice, it calmed me, not from relief, but with that drifting relaxation that comes only seconds after you know the worst has happened. It was a voice more animated than I had ever heard, the excited voice of a woman in full flight. It said everything, that voice, and everything I'd felt and thought on the way over went slack.

I stood outside the window for a moment, listening, but I couldn't stand it for long. I walked around the block, quickly, bought a newspaper at the variety store and when I returned she was off the phone. An arc of sweat darkened the underarms of her shirt.

"My mother called," Holly began. Something deflected off her face. "We had a near fight. You're right about her, you know . . ." She chatted on gaily, picked a grape from the bowl and popped it in her mouth. I put the newspaper down. I knew eventually she'd get to it, and when she stopped long enough to look at me, she recognized straightaway that something was wrong.

"Did *he* call *you?*" I asked.

She sat down on the bed.

"He called me back," she said.

Good old Holly. She never lied, even when you wanted her to.

"Come here," she said softly.

I could smell her, smell the sweat from the excitement of the phone call. I put my hands under her arms where it was warm and wet and I lifted her shirt off. She held her arms over her head and I pulled the shirt up over the top of them and her breasts came free and I licked each one. I did it with love, with inexpressible desire, and I knew it was the last time I'd be doing it.

She closed her eyes, she gave herself to it, I could taste tears on her cheeks.

"I love you," I whispered in her ear. "Promise me that you'll remember that. No matter what."

"I will," she said. "I promise."

And when it was over she sat on the side of the bed; she didn't cover herself.

"You have the most beautiful body I have ever seen in my life, Holly."

Her eyes welled up in tears, but she stopped them.

"Maybe if I were twenty-five . . ." she started, but I stopped her.

"I would have told you," she said. "It was only for lunch, but I would have told you."

"I know."

She laughed. It made me ache. "I wanted to wait till you came. You always take things better after you've come."

She went to the bathroom. I lay back on the pillows. I was facing the baseboard. I took a pencil from the desk and in very small letters I wrote on it: "Holly Briggs, I love you," and then I wrote the date.

I put on my clothes. She emerged from the bathroom. She wore the blue dressing gown. She raised my fingers to her lips.

"You still smell like me," she said. I kissed her softly on the lips; they were dry.

"Good-bye Holly," I said.

/15

*S*ummer came to an end; the weather
turned cold; women stepped outside on crisp fall evenings and
promptly went back inside for a sweater. Wind pumped the
trees, gave life a pinch, a hurry-up, made the shadows of leaves
dance on the church wall. It was knee sock and new eraser
weather, and it made me feel lucky again. I painted my apartment. I got a lucrative contract with the Ministry of Natural
Resources to write twelve speeches for the Minister. I never
heard from Nick Beach again, but, to quote him, no one is
indispensable. I did very well by my new friends at the vacuum
cleaner company. They wanted the audience on its feet at the
twenty-five minute mark, and, according to the cable I got
from Orlando, Florida, that's just what they got.

I didn't see Holly, not once, although one night I came
home and there was a kid, a runaway, sitting on my porch;
from the side he looked a bit like her.

Spolin got a job at a small theatre as playwright-in-residence but it went to his head. He started telling people to fuck off and they sacked him.

I stopped work on my "novel." I put it away. There's nothing wrong with writing with your dick in your hand, it's just that after you've come, you've got a hell of a lot of rewriting to do and I wasn't up for that.

I knew I didn't have a ghost of a chance of getting a woman, not for a while anyway, so I didn't try. I thought about looking up the henna-haired girl but I was still attached to Holly's body and I knew someone else's would feel obscene.

By now my cock was a red, frightened thing which leapt in alarm every time I unzipped my fly. I gave it a break too.

In early October, Zooey came to stay with me for two weeks while her mother went to Mexico. She'd fallen in love with an American, a former Green Beret who'd lost an eye in Vietnam. I called him Cyclops. Margaret thought that was passably funny. They had a rendezvous in Oaxaca.

One evening, Zooey and I were in the living room; she was reading a book called *How Boys See Girls* and I was tinkering with a speech on stocking Lake Ontario with hatchery-reared salmon. No one was going to jump to his feet after this one.

Zooey looked up from her book. "You know my sleepover?" she said. "I really want to have Alicia but her father won't let her have sleepovers during the week. Do you think it would be all right if I had Rachel?"

I was about to offer a lazy opinion when the phone rang.

"I've got a terrible hangover," a girl's voice began. "How about bringing me over a milk shake?"

"Holly," I said. "You got dumped again."

My daughter looked up. It's always the tone of voice that gives you away.

"They say a milk shake is good for a hangover," she continued. "It coats the stomach and puts sugar in the blood. I figured you'd know if it's true."

"It is true, Holly."

"So do you want to bring me one over?"

I laughed. "I can't tell you what a thrill it is that you've asked, but no, I can't."

"Have you got company or something?"

"Yes. I do."

"It's not you-know-who, is it?"

"No, Holly, it isn't."

"Then come over. Just for twenty minutes."

"I can't Holly. I really can't."

She paused, "You're very strong, Bix."

That night I dreamt about her: we were in deep tangled hedges outside my family cottage while inside, frightening men went from room to room, looking for us.

It was after four-thirty in the morning when the phone rang again. I didn't wait for a voice.

"Hello, Holly," I said.

I got dressed, I left a note for my daughter and because my car was in the garage, I pedaled her bike over to Melrose Avenue. The front window was open. I put my foot on the faucet and tumbled into Holly's bed. We didn't say anything, not for the longest time. Then she said: "I really want to come."

And when she did, I got dressed, still without a word. I opened the window and I stepped out into the bright fall air. It was almost morning and by the time I got home, you could hear sparrows in the churchyard next door.

About the Author

David Gilmour is a novelist and broadcast journalist. He was film critic for CBC-TV's *The Journal* and *The National* for over a decade, and was host of *Gilmour on the Arts*, a Gemini Award-winning arts talk show, for four years. He lives in Toronto and has two children, Jesse and Maggie.